Moving On

Stories by **DON KERSEY**

•

Cover Art and Book Design: Douglas Ensign

creative

LCCN: 2018911378
ISBN: 978-0-692-18767-8

Contents

Moving On

There were no lilacs in Miss Elsie's garden. There had been lilacs. She planted them herself back in 1946. The war was over. Her husband, Bucky, had not come home. God only knows what he was doing fighting in that war anyway. The army didn't really want colored men being war heros. Why did all those Negroes want to pick up a gun and risk their lives with a bunch of folks who didn't even want to sit beside them at a table? Elsie tried to convince herself it was because they wanted to protect their folks – the colored folks – at home. She sometimes believed it, like the times during the war when the air raid signal howled and she had to go around the house turning off lights and lowering the window shades. But when Bucky didn't come home....

She and Bucky Anderson had moved into this place right after they were married. Elsie was young then – twenty-two – and had what Bucky called 'a fine brown frame.' The frame was just a bit broader now, but at forty-five Elsie was still a handsome woman; tallish – almost five feet seven inches – and no noticeable gray in the hair that she still wore severely pulled back into a neat knot that rested primly on her neck. The wire-rimmed glasses she wore undercut the chic hairstyle and combined with Elsie's practical wardrobe gave her a spinster like appearance which probably accounted for everyone calling her 'Miss' Elsie. Bucky had talked the owner into letting them have the house on a lease-purchase plan. It was Bucky's idea. It turned out to be a good one. Elsie owned the house now. Of course, when they first moved in, it wasn't much of a house. The owner was probably glad to get rid of it. He was a white man with an old house in a colored neighborhood. Nobody was living in it. Bucky thought it had possibilities, but he wanted to own it before he started breaking his back fixing it up. Bucky started fixing it up. Elsie finished.

When Elsie's lilacs were in bloom people would stop outside her small front yard and just stand – inhaling the scent – sometimes moving from one bush to another and smiling as they picked up the differences in smell, sniffing the purple, then the pink. She was always afraid that people would break off a branch or two so they could take that lilac scent home with them, especially when she was away at work and there was no one to keep watch. But they never did. They just sniffed. They respected Miss Elsie and her lilacs.

Over the years those lilacs grew and grew. They didn't get much pruning. Elsie just let Mother Nature do what she does. The lilacs seemed to like that just fine. They grew big and bushy and every Spring rewarded Elsie with clusters of fragrant blossoms. It was in 1974 that Elsie thought maybe they were a little too bushy. While standing at her front gate she noticed that she could no longer see the small walkway leading to her rear entrance. She made a mental note to ask Deacon Wilson after church services on Sunday if he knew of anyone she could hire to cut the bushes back a bit. It was so hard to find anybody to do any work anymore. The young men who needed work didn't seem to want to do any-thing but stand around on the streets smoking God knows what. Deacon Wilson says they're smoking weed and up to no good. Elsie supposed the Deacon knew what he was talking about, but it was hard for her to picture some of those young men doing anything seriously wrong. A little devilment, maybe. After all, boys will be boys. Elsie knew most of them from church. Some of them sang on the youth choir. Of course, that was when they were growing up, when their mothers made them go to church. They were older now, made up their own minds. They no longer went to church. Mostly old men at church services now. Sometimes – those times when Pastor Lewiston was recycling some sermon that she had heard before – Elsie would look around the church and wonder what was going to happen when all the old men died off. Would the congregation be only women and young girls, and the only males those boys whose mothers made them go to church?

It was a Wednesday night. Elsie was coming home from a meeting of the Pastor's Aid Group. They were making plans for an upcoming Women's Day celebration at the church. The meeting lasted much longer than it should have. Hattie Fortson just wouldn't stop talking. She kept bringing up things that had nothing to do with Women's Day. She started harping on a sermon Pastor Lewiston preached at last year's Women's Day.

"That sermon was just not appropriate to Women's Day. What was all that preachin' about liars and cheaters and fornicators? What did that have to do with Women's Day?"

Truth is Hattie didn't really have any problem with the pastor's sermon until he started talking about church members who drank their liquor on Saturday nights and shouted 'hallelujahs' on Sunday morning. Hattie got kind of quiet when the preacher got to that part. She liked a little whisky in her Coca Cola when playing her Saturday night pinochle games with her lady friends and for Pastor Lewiston to question the righteousness of her innocent Saturday night backsliding, well.... He wasn't preachin'. He was meddlin'.

By the time Elsie walked up Darrah Street to her front gate it was almost eleven. Here it was her bedtime and she still hadn't ironed that blue blouse she planned on wearing to work the next day. She started up the three steps that led to her front door, opening her purse and fishing for the keys to the front door as she climbed. She noticed that there was no glow coming from the light at the back door. She always left it on when she went out. The glow from the light allowed her to see up the side walkway that led to the back door. She figured the bulb must have blown because she clearly remembered switching on that light. She heard the branches of the lilac bushes brush against each other, but Elsie hadn't really noticed any wind. She found her keys and easily flipped up the key to the front door. The little red dot she had pasted on the top of the key made it easy to identify as the key to the front door. The rear door key had a green dot. She inserted the key, turned it, then twisted the doorknob. As she pushed the door open she heard footsteps behind her, coming up the steps. Just as she turned to look two hands pushed her into the house. Someone else came from around the side of the house, ran to the door, came into the house and closed the door behind him.

Why do policemen ask the same question over and over? If she knew those two boys she'd tell the police who they were. She wasn't even sure they were boys. They could have been men. But the quick glimpse she got of the one that pushed her inside made her think he was maybe sixteen – maybe eighteen years old. But no – she didn't recognize him. Oh, he could have been one of those boys that hangs out on the corner up by the elevated train stop, but Elsie wasn't sure and she wasn't gonna send another Black man to prison unless she was sure it was a guilty one.

The one that had pushed her into the house pulled a sack down over Elsie's head so she couldn't see a thing. The other one grabbed her purse. A fat lot of good it was gonna do him. Elsie never carried more than twenty dollars and some change in her purse. Since she had stopped off at Willie's Diner after work for a meat loaf sandwich before she went to the Pastor's Aid meeting, she didn't even have that much. The one that took the purse was not happy. He kept asking Elsie where she kept her money. Kept wanting to know where she hid the cookie jar, as though Elsie would ever keep her money in a cookie jar. Cookie jars were for cookies. The Girard Trust Savings Bank was for money. Of course, they didn't believe her when she told them there was nothing of value in the house. The one who asked about the cookie jar actually pushed Elsie so hard she fell and hit her hip against the coffee table. The other one reprimanded him. It was almost as though he knew Elsie and cared about her. But then, if he cared about her, she wouldn't be on the floor by the coffee table with a sack over her head. The one who pushed her warned her that if she tried to take the sack off, she'd be sorry. Elsie stayed on the floor. She didn't know how much time passed. It didn't seem very long before she heard her front door open and close. She waited a few minutes to make sure they were gone, then she removed the sack and stood up. She was facing the television stand. There was only the stand. The television was gone. She looked into the dining room. Some doors were open on the sideboard and some stuff had been dumped on the floor. She lowered herself to the sofa and flinched at the pain she felt in her hip. She sat for at least fifteen minutes before she picked up the phone and dialed 911.

Elsie didn't go to work the next day. She had some sick leave saved up, so she wouldn't lose any pay. The policemen didn't leave until nearly two in the morning. They didn't think there was a good chance they would catch the two boys without an I.D. from Elsie, but they would do their best. One of them told her how lucky she was. Told her it could have been a lot worse. When she told Hattie, Hattie said, "Policemen always say that unless you're dead when they get there." Deacon Wilson came by and offered to find someone to thin out the lilac bushes – one of the neighborhood boys, but Elsie declined the offer. Deacon Wilson also checked the light by the back door. It was fine. Someone had just unscrewed the bulb. After the deacon left, Elsie walked up to the little shopping center by the elevated train station. She passed some young men who were standing on a corner in front of a White Castle, but she didn't turn to look at them. She went into the hardware store and bought a pair of heavy-duty garden shears. When she got home she started cutting down her lilac bushes. The pain in her hip slowed her down a bit, but it didn't stop her. She cut. She pulled. She yanked. When she did stop to go in to make herself some dinner, there were no lilacs in Miss Elsie's garden.

Memorial Day

"It's not easy being twelve years old." That's what my friend, Dave, said. I figured it was a lot easier for Dave than for me. For Dave, eleven was probably easier too. Thirteen would probably be easier too. If I hadn't known this on my own, which I did, Mom would certainly have reminded me.

"You goin' to the movies with that little white boy?"

"Mom, why do you always call David 'that little white boy'?"

"Because that's what he is. His mother probably calls you 'that little colored boy'. Least ways, let's hope that's what she calls you."

Dave and I went to the movies almost every Saturday afternoon. It cost twenty-five cents, a dollar if you were over twelve. I was kind of tall, so the cashier sometimes gave me a hard time.

"You're not thirteen yet?" Her tone indicated she expected my answer to be negative and untrue. "You're awf'lly tall for twelve."

I would protest and Dave would back me up. Then, as she had done many times before, the cashier would take my quarter and slide my ticket thru the little opening, but not without leaning in close to the rounded window of her booth so she could peek to make sure I wasn't crouching down to appear shorter than I really was. The cashier liked to wear those blouses that have bunched-up elastic all around the top so they can be worn off-the-shoulder, which is how she always wore them. When she leaned towards the window, the weight of her breasts (Dave called them "bazongers") forced the elastic to stretch and we could see what was barely hidden behind the cotton fabric. Dave said that's why she leaned forward.

"She knows how tall you are, Levon. She just wants us to look at her bazongers."

We always looked.

In 1950, you got a lot for your twenty-five cents at Philadelphia's Circle Movie Palace. You got to see cartoons, a chapter of whatever serial they were running and a full-length feature. The feature was usually a western or an Abbott and Costello movie – stuff like that. Sometimes they had contests. I once entered a Yo-Yo contest. If I hadn't messed up doing my 'over-the-falls' trick, I would have won first prize, a Schwinn bike. Dave didn't even make it through the preliminaries in the Yo-Yo contest, but he did get into a Little Rascals movie. Well, it wasn't the real Little Rascals. The movie theater held a talent contest, and the winners got to be in a movie based on The Little Rascals. You just had to go up on the stage and read the lines they gave you. There were three judges – they were called talent scouts – who decided which contestants would be the stars of tomorrow. Dave was a shoo-in. The judges loved him. He said his lines loud enough for the cashier out in her booth to hear him. And he was funny. He strutted about, periodically stopping to assume what he later told me was his 'Cary Grant pose'. He bobbed his head as he shouted the silly dialog, making the brown curls on his head bounce. Dave's curls were longer than any I'd ever seen on a boy, except in the movies. The curls, his grey eyes, his sharp features came together to give him a look which promised a striking, if not a handsome man.

I didn't enter that contest. I never really identified with Buckwheat.

At the Circle, the ushers didn't make you leave after the matinee. You could stay to see the regular feature. Dave and I almost always did. One Saturday, we sat through Destination Moon twice. There was hell to pay when we got home, especially for Dave. He had forgotten his grandmother was coming for dinner that Saturday, all the way from Atlantic City. Whenever Dave talked about his grandmother living in Atlantic City, I always pictured a big house set back on the beach and waves crashing against rocks that sat just at the end of a wooden walkway. That's the way beach houses looked in the movies. In reality, his grandmother lived in a small, frame house that wasn't anywhere near the beach. It wasn't even in Atlantic City. She lived in a place called Pleasantville. Pleasantville, New Jersey.

In my neighborhood, Memorial Day had ceremonial trappings to which we had to conform: parade, picnics, and for Dave and me, the most important, decorating our bikes. Actually, the day before the holiday was our decorating day. That way, the bikes were ready to ride on the next day, Memorial Day. My bike – not as nice as the one I should have won in the Yo-Yo contest – was blue and white, so the streamers of red, white, and blue ribbon, obligatory Memorial Day trim, really looked good hanging from the rubber handgrips at the end of the handlebars. They would look even better whipping out beside me as I pedalled as fast as I could down Tackawanna Street. A small American flag was taped to the center of the handlebars and three others jutted out from the back of the bicycle seat. Red, white, and blue-striped crepe paper was woven through the spokes of the wheels. Some of the kids liked to wrap crepe paper around the handlebars of their bikes, but I thought that was overkill. Dave agreed. We wanted to be cool, not junky. Somewhere, someone must have been thinking about honoring the war dead, but for the kids riding up and down Tackawanna Street, Dixon Street, Griscom Street and Meadow Street, patriotism was a well-decorated bicycle.

The order of the day was set. Bike riding, parade, picnic. The first two, Dave and I would do together, then we'd split up and head for the family picnics. My Mom spent the early part of the day preparing food for the picnic.

"Levon, don't you get so wrapped up riding up and down the streets with that little white boy that you forget to come out to the park to eat."

The park was Pennypack Park, where most of the colored families in the neighborhood went to have picnics. A few had family picnics in their backyard, but most of the yards were small. Pennypack was green and cool, and you could wade in the creek.

Mom was busy frying chicken and I could hear the grease popping in the pan. There would be crisp, fried chicken, potato salad made with little bits of sweet pickle, deviled eggs, and sweet, Kool-Aid punch. There would also be cakes, sweet potato pie, fruit and potato chips, but it was the chicken and potato salad that made it a picnic. I had put on my khaki pants, a blue, short-sleeved shirt, and my red U.S. Keds. Dave would be wearing his red Keds too. I wore white socks so I would be wearing all the colors of the day. I stood looking in the mirror that morning thinking how thin my arms looked hanging from the loose sleeves of the shirt. The movie theater cashier was right. I was tall. 'Gangly' was what Mom called me, but she always added, "You'll fill out when you get older. All of my side of the family fills out eventually." Everyone said I looked like Mom's side of the family. I thought I was more of a combination. I had Mom's nose, not flat, but prominent, and her strong chin. And I had Dad's eyes, with centers so dark they looked black. Most of Dad's relatives were big, too, so I guessed I would fill out – eventually.

My sister, Margret, came into the kitchen dressed for the parade. Margret belonged to The Hot Chocolates, a drill team that marched in all of the neighborhood parades. Margret was a precision marcher. She would have preferred being a majorette, but she couldn't master the art of baton twirling. However, she was good at the high-stepping moves, little kicks, fancy steps and pivots that precision marching required. She was particularly good at the hip-shakes that the girls added. (Margret's hips were already well on their way to fulfilling family tradition.) Mom gave Margret the once over.

"Since you've got on your marching clothes, I suspect I wont be getting any more help in the kitchen," she said.

"I've got practice before the parade," Margret answered. "I can't miss that."

Mom raised an eyebrow and pointed a finger at Margret's skirt. Margret tugged at the skirt, but the positioning of the hemline – safely above the knees, but dangerously close to the crotch – remained the same.

Margret didn't have any of my gangly qualities. She was a full-figured sixteen year-old. She had straightened her hair that morning and turned it under at the ends, I had seen the same hair style on June Allyson in some movie – not "Little Women," something else. Cute wasn't a word I often used when talking about Margret, but she did look cute with her navy-blue beret tilted to the side of her June Allyson hairdo. A red pom-pom sat in the center of the hat. The precision marchers also wore starched white, long-sleeved blouses, open at the neck so you could see their shiny, bright-red scarves. White boots and short, navy-blue skirts with wide, gold sashes tied at the waist completed the costume. It was Margret's skirt that held Mom's attention.

"Margret, is that skirt shorter than it used to be?"

"Of course not, Mom." Margret put her hands on her ample hips and gave her head a wanton toss, something Miss Allyson would never do. "I'm just taller. That's all."

Mom walked over and gave Margret's skirt a tug, hoping her tug would accomplish more than Margret's had. It didn't. "Just be careful you don't bend over," she said. "Every man watching the parade will be able to walk his eyes right through the valley of the shadow of death."

My mother was very inventive when it came to turning a Biblical phrase.

The parade was pretty much like it always was; lots of American Legion and VFW types carrying banners, the Boy Scout troop from the YMCA, a few decorated cars, and the string band from the Polish-American club. The Elks, the colored Masonic Lodge, also marched in the parade. The Big Elk – that's not what they called him, but I could never remember what they did call him – wore a funny hat with antlers. The first time I saw those antlers I thought they were growing out of the man's head. Of course, I was much younger then. The other elks wore funny hats, too, but without the antlers. My father had been a member of the lodge for as long as I could remember. Other than his job at the ball-bearing plant and occasional pinochle games, the lodge was the only thing that seemed to interest him. He didn't talk much about his job. The only time the SKF ball-bearing plant became a topic of conversation in the Tyler house was the second week of August each year when Daddy hauled us all off to the company picnic. The plant supplied all the food and drink, and there were games, and sometimes, rides for the kids. And there was music for dancing. I always liked these picnics because my father would parade me around and introduce me as "my boy, Levon." My father was six -feet tall and normally tipped the scales over the two-hundred mark. Some of his co-workers probably wondered when the loose-limbed boy at his side would begin to show a more pronounced resemblance to the Big Bill Tyler they knew. If they had looked into my eyes, they would have seen the resemblance already there.

The last group in the parade was The Hot Chocolates. Some of the older folks thought the drill team was a little too raucous for something as solemn as a Memorial Day parade, but, without a doubt, The Hot Chocolates were the most popular marchers in the parade. The Chocolates were a drum and bugle corp, majorettes, plus the precision marchers, which included my sister, Margret. Their sponsor was Miss Elsie Anderson. Miss Elsie taught piano and violin which explained her knowledge of music. I don't know where she learned precision marching. She was also a Daughter of the Eastern something or other, which was just another name for a lady Elk. I sometimes thought about learning to play the drums so I could join the drum and bugle corp, but I didn't want Dave to think I was looking for things to do without him.

As soon as the first syncopated rat-a-tat-tat from the drums bounced around the ears of the crowd, you could feel the mood of the parade-watchers change. Then the bugles would blast short, crisp notes. The notes sometimes sounded flat and out of tune, but it didn't matter. The bodies closest to the sounds were pulsing and feet were tapping to the beat of those drums. Dave – one of the few white faces in the crowd since most of the whites watched the parade on the other side of the Ave. before it crossed into our mostly colored neighborhood – was popping his head from side to side and marching in place. The majorettes were pushing their knees and their batons high into the air while the head majorette twirled her baton – first in front of her, then behind, then over her head, catching the sun on the silver-chrome bar. Then came the precision marchers; fifteen girls stepping, pausing, pivoting, and driving the crowd wild. Fifteen girls strutting with pride and a confidence that in the years to come – the turbulent sixties – would have them walking with pride in a very different kind of march.

After the parade, Dave stood throwing stones across the playing field at Roosevelt Junior High School. Gym classes used the field for playing football, baseball, soccer, and whatever else the gym teachers chose. The space wasn't suited to any of the sports, but it was what they had at Roosevelt, so it was what they used. Dave was hurling the stones with such force I was sure he was thinking of Mr. Bonnatucci, our phys. ed. teacher. Dave didn't like Bonnatucci; neither did I. Mr. Bonnatucci was always barking out orders.

"Hey Tyler." (Woof! Woof!) "That's right, you. Levon. That is your name, isn't it? Levon? Tyler? Move it. You can run faster than that."

How the hell did he know how fast I could run? Bonnatucci seemed to think all of the colored kids should be able to run really fast.

Dave had more reason to be pissed at Bonnatucci than I did. Our first week at Roosevelt, our first gym class, Bonnatucci came loping into the gym, barking, "It's time to see what you guys can do."

We did sit-ups and knee-bends and pull-ups and squat-thrusts till I thought I would drop. Just when we thought it was all over, Bonnatucci goes over to the wall and drops down the ropes.

"Start climbing." (Still barking.) He stood, waiting, but nobody moved, so he pointed at Dave. "You first."

Dave was exhausted, but he didn't want to let on in front of the entire class, so he went over to one of the ropes and hoisted himself up...and up...and up. I could see he was using every bit of strength he had left. All the while, Bonnatucci was down below, barking.

"Get it up there, Cooper, " he yelled. "Up."

It was after one of those yells that I saw Dave's feet lose their hold on the rope. A few seconds later, Dave came sliding down, his feet dangling and his hands scraping against the rope. No sound came from Dave's mouth, but I could see the scream on his face. I could see the pain. When Dave hit the floor, the pained look faded, and was replaced by an expression I had seen very few times before on his face. It was hate. I don't think Dave hated Bonnatucci because of the physical pain. No, it was the embarrassment. When Dave reached the bottom of that rope, he saw thirty-one adolescent faces staring at him. Thirty-one cocky boys momentarily subdued, standing in their ill-fitting white gym shorts and T-shirts, tugging at the foreign feel of their athletic supporters, thinking how easily it could have been one of them, rather than Dave, hitting the floor.

Dave threw one last stone, then came over to the steps where

I sat pulling at the grass that was growing between the cracks in the steps. Our bikes were propped against the railing. There was no one else on the field or around the school.

"Did you hear what happened to Chuckie Venango?" Dave was talking as he came towards the steps.

"What?"

"Bonnatucci called Chuckie's mother and told her about the tattoo on Chuckie's ass."

"How'd Bonnatucci find out about it?"

Dave sat on the steps. "Clint has gym with Chuckie," Dave answered. Clint said Bonnatucci saw Chuckie in the showers and noticed the tattoo. He thought Chuckie had some kind of disease. Bonnatucci is such a jerk. When he got a closer look, he saw it was a tattoo, so he hauled Chuckie off to the office and called Mrs. Venango."

I thought it was kind of stupid to put a tattoo of a snake on your behind, but it was even more stupid of the gym teacher to make such a fuss. He must have known it wasn't a real tattoo, the kind that never comes off. "I bet Bonnatucci will be checking behinds in the shower room for the rest of the term," I said.

Dave, always looking for a way to toss a dig at Bonnatucci, added, "Didn't you know? That's how he gets his jollies."

The parade had been over for at least two hours, but Dave and I were still hanging out. We knew it was time to split up and head for our separate picnics, but just like the year before, and the year before that, we were putting it off.

"Hey, Levon," Dave had his left foot braced on the pedal of his bike and was swinging his right leg high and wide over his bike to mount up, much like we had seen Roy Rogers do with Trigger on many Saturday afternoons at The Circle, "why don't you stop by my house and have a hot dog before you ride out to Pennypack?"

It sounded like a good idea to me. Dave's house was closer than the park and I was hungry.

"Sure thing," I answered.

We'd been friends since the fourth grade; that's when Dave's family moved here from Kensington, which is just another part of Philadelphia, and Dave transferred to my school. All that time, we never really did family type things together. Oh, I had lunch at Dave's a couple of times before going to the movies, and Dad let me invite Dave to the SKF picnic one year, but that was about all. This would be the first time either had invaded the other's Memorial Day picnic.

Dave's house was the corner house on his block, so we could go right into the back yard through the side gate, without going through the house.

"Levon," Mrs. Cooper always pronounced my name with the accent on the 'von,' "come right in."

Dave's mother looked and sounded like she should be dressed like Judy Garland's mother in "Meet Me In St. Louis." That day, she was wearing bright green slacks and a green blouse that had pineapples on the sleeves. She wore a wide, white belt around her waist. All in all, I preferred my fantasy look for Mrs. Cooper.

Chuckie Venango was there with his folks, and he ran to the gate as soon as he saw us come in. Chuckie had catsup stains on the front of his mighty mouse T-shirt. It looked like Mighty Mouse had a bloody nose. Chuckie's father was already bombed on Schlitz. (According to Chuckie, Schlitz was the only beer Mr. Venango would drink.) There were some other kids there, but I didn't recognize them, so I supposed they were relatives. Mrs.

Cooper gave us hot dogs and told us to help ourselves to something to drink. We slopped our dogs with mustard and relish. I could hear some women talking about what happened on the last episode of "The Guiding Light," and some man was waving his arms and telling a guy in Navy whites that Truman was going to ship our boys to Korea. I bit into the juicy hot dog, and the roll started to crumble. Dave and Chuckie laughed. I was coping with the mush in my mouth when Mr. Venango's voice cut through the other sounds in the yard.

"We don't go to that part of the park anymore. The niggers have taken it over."

I was going to ignore it. In my head, I told myself, "ignore it." After all, it wasn't the first time I'd heard the word; not even close to the first time, but I didn't expect to hear it here – not at Dave's house. Chuckie was looking towards the big washtub filled with ice, bottles of beer, and sodas, where his father stood, uncapping a bottle of Schlitz. Dave was looking at me. I recognized the voice of Bing Crosby floating out of the radio which sat just inside the kitchen window.

"...dear hearts and gentle people,
That live in my hometown..."

Mr. Venango was still talking. "We used to go out to Penny-pack a lot. Did you know there are fish...." I heard his voice saying other things, but inside my head everything translated to "The niggers have taken it over." (*Ignore it.*) My father had said the same thing. "I tell you, Levon, the niggers have just about taken over Pennypack." It didn't mean anything when Dad said it. (*Ignore it.*)

Mrs. Cooper patted me on the shoulder. She was saying something in her Meet-Me-In-St.-Louis voice. I forced my ears to gather in her words.

"Don't pay any attention to him, Levon. He's had too much to drink. Besides, you know we don't think of you that way." *(What way?)* "Why, you spend so much time with Davey, we don't even think of you as colored." *(Let's hope that's what she calls you.)* "You know what I mean." *(No. I don't.)*

I tried to swallow the food still in my mouth. Dave was quiet, but I recognized the look on his face. It was the same silent scream I had seen there as he slid down the rope in the gymnasium, and I watched it fade away, just as I had watched it disappear in the gymnasium. I waited for what I was sure would follow. I waited for the hate. I waited to see the hate find its target at the ice-filled tub, the way it had zeroed in on Bonnatucci that day in the gym. Instead I saw Dave's face soften.

"Get us some sodas, Chuckie," Dave said.

Dave turned back to me, and I thought I saw a slight smile. *(Where's the hate, Dave?)* Chuckie came back carrying three root beers. Dave took two and handed one to me. *(You trying to console me, Dave? Don't. Just hate Mr. Venango, Dave. He burned me, just as surely as those ropes burned you.)* The bottle of root beer was cold against my hand. Water dripped from the bottle on to my Keds, leaving little dark spots on the red canvas. *(Hate him, Dave. Do it for me. Hate him. Do it.)*

"...dear hearts and gentle people
Will never, ever let you down."

(Shut up, Bing. What do you know about the people who "live and love in my hometown?")

The mustard on my hot dog was the yellow kind. I preferred the spicy, brown mustard. It stings the tongue sometimes, but I still liked it. I wished for some spicy, brown mustard. The yellow stuff was going to make me vomit.

Most of the people who had come to the park were already packed and gone. Mom and Dad were still playing pinochle with Miss Parthy and Mr. Seth. It was dark, and it was difficult to see the markings on the cards. The flashlights Mr. Seth had strung between two trees were of little help.

"...ten, eleven, twelve...." Mom was counting. "We did it. We made it. Fourteen plus twenty-one meld plus one-hundred-eighteen makes one-fifty-three. We did it again, Parthy. We beat 'em."

Mom and Miss Parthy were playing as partners against Mr. Seth and Dad. They almost always beat the men. Dad said Mom and Miss Parthy had signals between them. He never said they cheated, but he made it known he felt they had set up an unfair advantage. Since Mom and Miss Parthy seemed to win a lot, no matter whom they played, it seemed Dad had a point. Miss Parthy said it was just luck.

"I've always been lucky at cards." she said.

Mr. Seth was taking Miss Parthy home, so he folded her card table and two of the chairs – the other two were ours – and put them into his car. Dad and I carried our stuff over to our Black Plymouth. Cars spinning up dust from their wheels as their drivers sped too fast down the dirt road leading into the park had left a coating of tan mist on the Plymouth. I knew that Dad would clean the car the next morning before he sat down to breakfast and it would be as shiny as Mom's patent leather pumps. Margret was gone, preferring to walk home with her best friend, Brenda. While Dad was maneuvering the folding chairs in the back seat of the car to make room for the lounge chair Mom had insisted on bringing to the park, Mom reached her right arm around my shoulders and pulled me to her side. It annoyed me if she did this when other people were around, but I loved to have her do it when no one else could see. I felt comfortable and protected. She held me there, then, suddenly pointed to the sky.

"Look. A shooting star."

I looked in just enough time to see the traveling light disappear.

"That's another soul escaping from purgatory," she said.

"What's purgatory?" It sounded like a religious thing, but I had never heard Reverend Coles talk about purgatory in any of his sermons at the Second Baptist Church, so I guessed it was something Mom picked up from one of her Creole relatives.

"It's kind of a stopping off place where you get little punishments while you're waiting to be let into Heaven."

"Only one soul gets out for each shooting star?" I asked. "Just one?"

Mom looked puzzled. "I guess so."

"You don't see many shooting stars."

"No, Levon. I guess you don't."

I guess purgatory can last a long, long time.

Freedom Trained

Caroline dipped her right index finger into the coconut oil, rubbed her finger across the palm of her left hand, rubbed her palms together, then smoothed the oil over her hair. She avoided getting the oil on her forehead. She didn't want to sprout any tiny pimples. Pimples became zits. Zits could leave scars and any kind of blemish seemed to take forever to fade on her cocoa-colored skin. She picked up her brush and with a firm grip on the handle carefully brushed her hair back from her face till it was smooth and taut from forehead to crown (she had just touched up the edges with the hot comb), then she caught the hair at the back – thick, black curls – with a circular comb and let the hair hang – almost a ponytail, but not quite. She liked wearing her hair this way. She thought it feminine without being fussy. Ann would not agree.

Caroline Ford and Ann Dixon had been roommates since their sophomore year at Howard University in D.C. After graduation they had taken a five-room apartment above an art supply store in Philadelphia, Ann's hometown. The apartment was cheap and in need of work. Caroline thought the neighborhood needed work too, but Ann talked it up as 'the only place to live in Philly.' What Caroline thought bizarre, Ann called funky.

Just steps from their apartment on Fourth Street was South

Street, the main neighborhood thoroughfare, and it was dotted with storefronts converted from furniture stores, bridal shoppes and cheap junk stores into craft shops, funky (Ann's word) cafés and expensive junk stores. The mix of people was just as eclectic as the mix of buildings. There were old residents who were unable or unwilling to leave, new residents looking for cheap housing and loose surroundings, and a sprinkling of entrepreneurs whose instincts told them the neighborhood was going to be hot, so it was worth their while to wait out the transition period.

Caroline's parents in Virginia had assumed that she would be coming back to Richmond to teach school when she graduated. Caroline had assumed the same until Ann convinced her that being so close to her parents would 'smother her creativity.' The fact that Ann's parents lived in Philadelphia didn't seem to matter. (They actually lived in someplace called Yeadon, which Ann described as 'another world' and she vowed that she would neither see nor communicate with her parents any more regularly than Caroline would with her parents in Richmond. Also, Ann felt Caroline was much more influenced by parental opinion than she. Not true. If it were true, Caroline would be living in Richmond.)

Caroline could hear Ann dragging her bicycle up the stairs. The door opened and closed.

"I smell burnt hair."

Ann had an afro and never missed an opportunity to chide Caroline about her straightened hair. However, minute for minute on a daily basis Ann spent more time picking, conditioning and shaping her fro than Caroline spent brushing back and pinning up her curls. Caroline had never seen Ann's hair in any other style. Although she was sure Ann hadn't grown up wearing politically correct hair, she sometimes pictured her in a crib, her diaper drooping down around her knees and her hair in a perfectly shaped globe around her head.

"When are you going to free yourself from that hot comb and let those naps do what they want to do? You don't know how much more fun it is to take a shower when you don't have to worry about getting your hair wet."

Since the apartment had no shower – only a tub – this was a moot point. They had discussed putting in some sort of shower in the tub but decided against it since the living arrangement was only temporary. They planned to move as soon as they both got more or less permanently settled into jobs. After ten months in Philadelphia Caroline was still substitute teaching and Ann was waiting tables at Café Eyes. Ann had been offered a very good job with IBM but decided it demanded too much conformity. She turned it down.

"How much is too much?"

"I'd rather work at Café Eyes until the right job comes along."

Ann could really work at whatever she chose. Caroline sometimes questioned Ann's ability to use common sense, but she envied Ann's intelligence. Ann always made the Dean's List and still found time to be active in every campus cause she deemed worthy of her time.

"You know Caroline, you would really look stunning with your hair close-cropped. You've got the face for it. I was talking about it with Loyetta at the café and she agreed. It would be damn sexy."

"For Christ's sake, will you lay off my hair?"

It was April 1970. The hip generation – "hippies" to the general population – were well represented in Philadelphia and a familiar sight in the South Street neighborhood. Bell-bottoms, fringed vests, gauzy, Indian-style shirts and anything tie-dyed were wardrobe essentials. The war in Vietnam plodded on, Frank Rizzo was still Philadelphia's police commissioner, and Philadelphia along with a large portion of the world was preparing to celebrate the first Earth Day.

"Ira Einhorn is speaking at the Earth Day celebration." Ann's reaction to Caroline's information was a minor grunt. Caroline continued, "Are we going on our own or as part of a Café Eyes contingent?"

"Whichever."

"Am I detecting a slight lack of enthusiasm? Saving the planet should be right up your alley."

"Good cause, but…"

"But?"

"Not sure I need to hear a drug-loving preacher of free love talk to me about saving trees."

"Wow. Where did that come from?"

"Don't get me wrong, the movement is a good thing. But right now, it could pull attention away from civil rights issues. In America, we need to think about saving people, not trees."

"Loyetta's been giving you the Huey Newton pep talk again."

"I don't need a pep talk. And you shouldn't either. It's time for us to let go of that sorority girl shit and do some real good for the world."

"Excuse me, but who bugged me to pledge and become an Alpha?"

On April 22 Ann and Caroline joined a huge crowd in Fairmount Park to listen to speakers that included Edmund Muskie and Ralph Nader and Ira Einhorn. Loyetta decided not to go.

David Fierman was born in Ohio. He spent his college fresh-man and sophomore years at Kent State then transferred to Temple University because he wanted to go to Temple's Law school. He also wanted to put some distance between himself and his parents. Having loving parents – and Shirley and Irv Fierman were loving parents – carries a burden of guilt for accepting their love – and their financial support – and not being able to fit into the niche they're carving out for you. At Temple University he would still have their love – and financial support – but fewer recriminations; ergo, less guilt.

David worked part-time at Café Eyes. He and Loyetta were an item for about a minute and a half, then Loyetta got involved prepping for the Revolutionary People's Constitutional Convention and decided it was not cool to be hooked up with a Jewish pre-law student from Ohio while handing out leaflets touting 'If you're not part of the solution you're part of the problem.' David was taking a few days off to go back to Ohio where he planned to join some of his old classmates in what he said was going to be a major demonstration at Kent State protesting Nixon's Cambodian campaign. The protest was on a Monday, so he thought he would fly back to Philly on Monday night missing only one day of classes at Temple. Caroline offered to cover his shifts at the café.

On the morning of May 5th, a light fog had settled over center city Philadelphia. The WCAU-TV weatherman was predicting a warm day – low seventies. The fan-shaped leaves on the gingko tree planted at the edge of the sidewalk in front of Café Eyes were Spring-green. Across the street from the café, Sheila Zimmer was unlocking the door of her ladies-wear store where she would spend her day arranging and rearranging her supply of garments that very few ladies of the new South Street would ever consider wearing; but Sheila was content to sell a bra or a pair of panties now and then. At 72, Sheila wasn't there to make money. Her husband, Henny owned the building free and clear and when Henny died he left Sheila 'not rich, but very comfortable' (Sheila's words). She and her one employee – Mary Kate Scoletto, a sixty-year-old single lady who lived in South Philly – worked the store four days a week – Monday thru Thursday. Sheila was closed on Fridays and Saturdays (because Henny would want that) and opened late on Sundays (so Mary Kate could go to Mass). When Mary Kate got to the store on that mild Tuesday in May, she and Sheila would have coffee and spend the first part of their day talking about the tragedy at Kent State. "Four people killed. How many others hurt?"

"All of the parents must be worried sick."

"What were those men thinking? Just shooting like that?"

"Those young people were just saying they don't like war. You don't shoot people for saying they don't like war."

Above the art supply store on Fourth Street, Ann, Caroline and Loyetta sat around the small kitchen table. Ann and Caroline each cradled coffee cups. Loyetta sat drumming her fingers on the gray Formica tabletop.

"Loyetta, you keep that up, you're gonna break a nail."

Loyetta looked at Ann but didn't stop drumming, so Caroline gently placed her hand over Loyetta's and the drumming ceased.

"If he were alright, David would have called. He knows we were expecting him back last night."

Caroline removed her hand. "Things must be crazy out there, Loyetta. Maybe he just hasn't had a chance to call. He's probably with his parents."

Loyetta was still looking at Ann. "What do you think?"

No one from Philly made the trip to Ohio for David's services. In keeping with their faith, the Fiermans buried their son as soon as the circumstances would allow. There was a small memorial service at Café Eyes for David's Philadelphia friends. David was a Jimi Hendrix fan so Loyetta had several Hendrix albums on hand. She got to play them all again as a memorial to Hendrix in September of that same year when Hendrix closed his eyes for good, saying goodbye to life at the ripe old age of twenty-seven, just six years older than David when he had his eyes closed for him by an overzealous man in riot gear.

Loyetta Simmons spent nearly two semesters at Temple University. She was no genius in high school, but her grades were good and a well-meaning guidance counselor had steered her towards some scholarship money and assured her that she could be 'a credit to her race.' She had no real course of study; she was just fulfilling the university's first year requirements. It was in her second semester while taking what was labeled a General Studies class and listening to Assistant Professor Iris Jacobs lecturing on the link between folk music and campus unrest that Loyetta decided she needed to be something other than a credit to her race. So, in May of 1967 she moved out of her parent's house in Southwark and into a studio on Rodman Street and began to seek out ways to 'make a difference.' To pay the rent on the Rodman Street apartment she took a job waiting tables and working the cash register at Café Eyes. The owner quickly saw that Loyetta had a real knack for the business. She was efficient and had a sassy attitude that he thought added to the appeal of the café. Business was already good, but it got better. Eighteen months later, Loyetta was given the title 'Assistant Manager.'

It was in November of her first year at Café Eyes that Loyetta got her first chance to make a difference. A student demonstration was planned in favor of including Black History courses in public schools. Loyetta had planned on joining the demonstration but got detained at the café covering for someone who was late arriving for her shift. News reports that night showed the students being routed by Philadelphia police, an attack called for by police commissioner Frank Rizzo. The next day, Loyetta was part of a group carrying placards and marching in North Philadelphia denouncing the commissioner.

The summer after David's death, Loyetta spent most of her free time working with a group at the Church of the Advocate preparing for the Revolutionary People's Constitutional Convention. The plenary session was scheduled for September 5th at Temple University and the church had opened its doors for those registering for the convention. At times, she was so busy she wondered if her job was getting in the way of her doing more to 'make a difference.' But she needed her job and just as importantly, she liked her job. On the Saturday before the convention a Philadelphia police officer was shot in Fairmount Park. Although there was no proven connection between the killing and the People's Revolutionary Convention or the Black Panther Party, the police commissioner called for a raid of the Panther headquarters. Heavily armed officers strip-searched and arrested party members in North Philadelphia, Germantown and West Philadelphia. The following week the convention went on as planned, attended by a far larger crowd then was expected. Loyetta was there. Ann was there. Caroline was not there. Loyetta knew that she would not be going to the upcoming gathering in Washington, so she took in as much as she could at the Philadelphia convention. When it was over, she thought about all that had happened in the last three years of her life and she wondered if being a credit to your race might be easier than trying to make a difference.

Caroline was offered a permanent job teaching History at a junior high in Northeast Philadelphia. The prospect of a regular paycheck prompted her to suggest to Ann that they be on the look-out for an upgrade in their living conditions. The plenary session of the RPC convention in Philadelphia was the preamble to the full convention being held in November in Washington, D.C. Ann was making plans to attend and wanted to hold off looking for a new place until the end of the year.

"Before upgrading my living conditions, I may need to upgrade my income. And you need some time to make sure that junior high school thing is going to work out. Junior high? Carrie, those kids can get on your last nerve. You still planning on going to Richmond for Thanksgiving?"

"Yes. I'm really sorry I can't come to the convention with you."

"The convention starts the day after Thanksgiving. You could come for the weekend."

"Oh, sure. My parents will be thrilled when I hop up from the table – 'No time for pie. Got to meet Ann in D.C.' – And you know I have to be back for classes on Monday."

"And I know your parents wouldn't approve of you..."

"Don't go there," Caroline interrupted.

"They're like my parents," Ann continued. "They think their membership in the NAACP is changing the world. No personal investment necessary."

Caroline was silent for several minutes. "Sometimes the personal investment is too much. For Dave's parents, it was too much, don't you think?"

Come January, there was a change in living conditions. When she returned from the convention in D.C. Ann informed Caroline that she was going to enroll in a master's program at Howard.

"Caroline. You wouldn't believe how disorganized those people were in D.C. There wasn't enough meeting space; schedules were screwed up; just crazy. We need leaders, Caroline. Politics! That's where I'm headed. I know I'm not giving you a lot of notice, but I spoke to the admissions people while I was in Washington and I think they're going to let me do the Spring semester."

When Caroline went home for Christmas, she told her parents she would be coming back to Richmond at the end of the school year.

Bicentennial fever was running high in Philadelphia in June of 1976. July fourth was just around the corner. Celebrations! Fireworks! Patriotism! And oh, so many tourists. Queen Elizabeth was crossing the Atlantic to give the city a Bicentennial Bell inscribed with the words 'Let Freedom Ring' even though the Queen was surely aware that the Americans in attendance at the presentation were celebrating their freedom from her colonial ancestors. President Ford would be giving a speech. He would soon have his freedom from the presidency when Jimmy Carter replaced him in the oval office. And wonder of wonders – Moses was on the bill of fare. Charlton Heston – though not in his Ten Commandments' robes – would be in town to part the crowds on Independence Mall. Yes, the Bicentennial Bounties were many. But on this particular Saturday in June of 1976 Loyetta Simmons, Caroline Ford and Ann Dixon were meeting in Philadelphia for another celebration. Community activist Ann Dixon was planning a move back to Philadelphia to run for the Pennsylvania State Assembly.

"Loyetta, don't you think a celebration now is a little presumptuous?"

"Hell, no, Ann. You're gonna win, if not this time, then the next. Like it or not, you are gonna be a credit to your race and make a difference for all of us. So, get your butt on that train out of D.C. Caroline will be here Friday night."

Caroline did arrive on Friday night. Ann arrived by noon on Saturday. By two o'clock the three women sat in Café Eyes trading stories: Loyetta telling about her plans to buy into the business and eventually become part owner of Café Eyes, Caroline gushing with excitement over her students in Richmond and work with the local NAACP branch, Ann soberly relating her experiences in Washington and her doubts about returning to Philadelphia.

Caroline reached around and fingered her hair, still pulled back in her feminine but practical ponytail. She leaned in to Ann and said, "Any woman with that perfect circle of hair can't have any doubts."

Ann laughed. "For Christ's sake! Will you lay off my hair?"

All In A Day's Work

Bernie stood at the kitchen sink licking cream cheese off his fingers. Crumbs from his just finished sesame bagel were sprinkled over the front of his shirt, mostly on that part covering the paunch bulging over his belt, a roll of flesh that now seemed to be a permanent part of his physique. He usually had his breakfast at the deli that he owned with his brother Sol, but Sol volunteered to open up on his own today so that Bernie could get a little extra shuteye. Bernie was the older brother – by six years. He celebrated his 65th birthday eight months ago. Since then, Sol has been treating him like he might keel over at any moment.

"Bernie, leave those cases be. The delivery guy will get them. You want to have a heart attack?"

Paunch to the contrary, Bernie still felt as strong as an ox. He gets a little tired when he has to double shift at the deli, but who doesn't? Sixty-five or thirty-five, you work hard, you get tired.

Shirley came into the kitchen carrying a mesh laundry bag. "Bernie, sit down, why don't you? Eat at the table. That's what it's for."

"I'm finished eating."

"You left your towel hanging over the shower door and the bathroom sink is full of stubble. You cleaned your electric razor over the sink and left it full of stubble. It's Thursday. You know Mabel comes on Thursdays."

"Yeah. She's coming to clean the house. I thought that included the bathroom."

"You know I like to straighten things up before she gets here."

"But then there's nothing for Mabel to do. Are you trying to put her out of a job?"

"There's plenty for her to do. But I don't want her to think we're slobs. It was different when the kids were still here. There was an excuse. With just the two of us, what's the excuse?"

"Excuse for what?"

"I'll bet Mabel's house is so clean you could eat off the floors."

Bernie formed a mental picture of Mabel – who had to be almost as old as he (though she didn't look it) – sitting cross-legged on the floor having dinner. No matter how clean the floor, he couldn't imagine Mabel doing that. Bernie often wondered why Mabel continued to come out to Bala Cynwyd to clean their house. Shirley told him that it wasn't the money. Mabel could live comfortably on her dead husband's social security and pension. When she first started working for Shirley it was to bring in a little extra money because work was a little slow at the factory where her husband Dell was employed. When things picked up for Dell, Mabel planned to stop doing day's work, but Shirley convinced her to keep coming until her kids were out of the house. Both kids were long gone, but Shirley and Mabel both avoided the topic of ending the relationship.

"Did you remember to bring home some brisket from the deli last night?

"It's in the right-hand vegetable drawer of the fridge."

"Good. Mabel really likes your brisket. We're going to

have it for lunch."

Bernie took one last gulp of coffee. "Gotta go. I'll be closing up tonight so Sol can leave a little early. Why don't you come over to the deli around seven and we can have dinner together?"

"That sounds good. Gives me an excuse not to spend the evening with Marilyn Zimmer. Her husband is out of town and she's looking for company. She'll want to go to some trendy restaurant where she'll order what she's heard is good and then not eat it because it's too fattening."

"Why do you need an excuse?"

"Well, I feel bad for her. I think her husband goes away on business because he doesn't like her anymore than I do. And ever since her son, Stu, married that Vietnamese girl, Marilyn can't talk about anything else. It's always 'What are they going to do about the kids?' There are no kids, and Stu and his wife are so tied up with their careers I doubt if there ever will be."

Bernie kissed Shirley on the top of her head. "I'm out of here. Call me if you decide to go trendy instead of coming to the deli."

"I will."

"See ya."

Mabel got off the C bus at City Line Avenue and walked the two blocks up to the street that led to the cul-de-sac where Shirley and Bernie Berman lived. As she turned the corner she noticed the smell of cooking oil. She figured it had to be coming from the McDonald's on the other side of City Line Avenue. At the end of the block she turned into Tea Rose Lane, which didn't smell like roses but there was no more eau de McDonald's. The Bermans lived in the second house in so Mabel didn't have to walk to the end of the turn-a-round. Like all the other houses on Tea Rose Lane, the Berman house was a raised ranch with a sloping lawn. Tasteful shrubbery lined the top of the slope, not because Bernie Berman cared about gardening, but the neighborhood watch committee made your life hell if your lawn and plantings weren't in keeping with the visual scheme of Tea Rose Lane.

Both Bermans talked about moving into an apartment and giving up the headaches of dealing with a house. If Bernie stopped working in the deli, they would probably do it. If they did, Mabel would have her Thursdays free, just like her other days, which would make her daughter, Clarissa, happy. "Momma, why do you still go out there to work for that woman? " Clarissa always referred to Shirley Berman as 'that woman.' It made Shirley sound like a character Bette Davis might play in one of her films. "You don't have to work. Stay home. Enjoy life. Be a colored lady of leisure." Mabel had six other days in the week to enjoy life. Thursdays with Shirley Berman was not a deal-breaker when it came to enjoying life. Since the two Berman girls had gone – one married with two children and the other divorced with a house in Connecticut, a Mercedes and a Sable coat – there was little for Mabel to do. Mabel suspected that Shirley spent Wednesday evenings straightening out everything in the house because when she arrived on Thursday it was as neat as a pin. And once there, Mabel barely had time to do a little dusting and run the vacuum, maybe change the towels in the main bathroom. She couldn't do anything until she and Shirley had their first cup of coffee and a Danish. Then, before she could get her hands on a bottle of Pine Sol, Shirley was calling her for lunch. (Bernie's deli had the best brisket.) Right after lunch, it was time to watch All My Children. They would spend the rest of the afternoon hashing through the lives of the residents of Pine Valley.

Shirley saw Mabel coming up the walkway and opened the door.

"Coffee's ready, Mabel. Come on in."

Mabel closed the door behind her, put her coat in the hall closet and headed for the kitchen. "And how is Miss Shirley today?"

"You do that just to irritate me, don't you?"

Mabel lifted a cup from the cabinet and put on her most innocent face. "Do, what, Miss...."

"My name is 'Shirley.' My mother did not name me 'Miss Shirley,' so you will kindly call me by my correct name. "

"You know, I forget, Mi..."

"Mabel Carter. You can be an evil woman when you want to be."

They laughed, got their coffee and sat down at the kitchen table to pick over the cheese and pineapple Danish.

Bernie sat at the counter nibbling on half of a pastrami sandwich. He wasn't really hungry; in fact, he was feeling a little nauseous. He had Earl make him half of a sandwich because Sol had said he looked like he needed some nourishment.

"Sit down and eat something. You look tired and washed out. And you're sweating like a pig."

Earl Mobley came to work at the deli about two years after Sol and Bernie opened the place. They depended on Earl almost as much as they depended on each other to run the place.

"Something wrong with the pastrami, Bernie? You're not eating."

"It's fine, Earl. My stomach is a little queasy. I'll get a little seltzer."

Bernie drank a full glass of seltzer. After forcing a belch, he went to the freezer and pulled out a carton of frozen French fries. His next memory was of Earl bending over him and calling for Sol to 'get over here.'

Mabel had gone to the service at Heavenly Comfort Memorial funeral home, but she didn't go to the cemetery. Clarissa called that night. "Just wanted to make sure you got home all right." Clarissa had a good heart. She really wanted life to be easy for her mother. She got Mabel a rocking chair last Christmas. Mabel always remembered to sit in the chair at least once every time Clarissa was in the house.

"Well, Momma, I guess Shirley Berman will be looking for that apartment now. Or maybe her daughter in Connecticut will want her to come live with her. God knows she's got the space."

"They just put Bernie in the ground and you've already got the poor woman out in the street."

"Momma, you know that's not what I meant."

"Yes, Clarie, I do know. I also know what you did mean."

"Well, I won't lie. No disrespect to Mr. Berman. I'm sure he was a fine man, but you know how I feel about your running out to Bala Cynwyd."

"I know how you feel, and I know you mean well. I love you, Clarie."

"Love you right back, Momma."

Shirley's daughter, Linda – the divorced one – had convinced Shirley to limit the hours the family would be sitting shiva. Sol had been a bit of a stumbling block. "You know how long we've had the deli? Lots of people will want to come pay their respects." Though she didn't voice it to Sol, Shirley was relieved that Linda had prevailed. She sat, and she listened.

"So sorry for...."

"This must be so difficult for...."

"If there's anything I can do for...."

Sol's wife, Dottie came by everyday. She always sat on the same low stool, looking uncomfortable. She probably was very uncomfortable. Dottie had gained quite a few pounds in middle age and the stool disappeared under her black-skirted bottom. Shirley leaned in towards Dottie.

"Dottie, why don't you go have something to drink?"

"You know, I think I'll do that."

Dottie got up from the stool and Shirley thought both Dottie and the stool welcomed the break. Shirley noticed a smudge on the tan carpeting right in front of the big armchair where Bernie liked to sit with a mug of hot chocolate reading one of those horror novels that he liked so much. (Stephen King and Dean Koontz were two favorites.) That smudge was from some chocolate he spilled. She and Mabel had tried to get rid of that stain. They had succeeded only in turning a dark smudge into a light smudge. Shirley remembered they had moved the chair to cover the stain. As she sat waiting for the next person to come offer condolences she wondered who moved the chair and uncovered the stain. The unlocked front door opened. Shirley immediately recognized the woman coming in. The woman paused and looked at the basin and pitcher of water that sat on a small table in the entranceway. There was a moment of puzzlement, then she picked up the pitcher and holding her hands over the basin she poured the tepid water over her hands. She wiped her hands on the towel provided and then looked at Shirley. Her look relayed a question. 'Did I do that right?' Shirley smiled. The woman walked over to Shirley stopping briefly to acknowledge the other family members. Both daughters stood and embraced the woman. Shirley still smiled.

"I cannot tell you how happy I am to see you."

And the woman answered, "It's Thursday. Where else would I be?"

Under The Silence

Tennessee Williams
A Separate Poem

He

It's Saturday. I could really stay in bed a little longer. It feels good to be under this comforter. I think it must be new. It seems fluffier than I remember. In any case, it feels good. I don't remember Kate mentioning that she bought a new comforter. That doesn't mean she didn't mention it. It just means that I don't remember her mentioning it. I could ask her, but she might think I wasn't paying attention when she mentioned it — if she did mention it. I can hear Kate in the kitchen. She's probably making coffee. I'll smell it soon. That's one of the good things about our moving into this condo — everything on one floor. You make coffee in the kitchen, you can smell it in the bedroom. The ceiling fan is going. I'm pretty sure it wasn't on when we went to bed. Kate must have gotten up in the middle of the night and turned it on. She's been doing that lately.

She says she gets hot, starts sweating. She's fifty-two. I guess I know what's going on. Hot flashes? Don't know why she bothered with a new comforter. Every morning it's all on my side of the bed. Maybe she got it for me. She's thoughtful. But it's almost April; how much longer will I need it? Well, if the hot flashes go on for a while, Kate might get heavy-handed with the air conditioning and I could need the comforter all summer long. She's a planner. Before we moved into this condo — at the house in Jenkintown (that's in Pennsylvania) — I would work in the garden after breakfast on most Saturdays. Can't say I miss that. When we first moved into the house keeping the front garden looking good was a matter of pride. It didn't take long for it to become a chore. If we had had a son, I probably would have turned over some of the work to him, but we only had the one child — Trish, a daughter — and we didn't want our little princess digging in the dirt.

She

I think I hear Gary. It's Saturday. He should sleep a little longer, but he wont. He still gets up as though he has to tend the garden like he did at the house — before we moved into this condo complex. I think he misses working in the garden. People who work in offices like getting their hands dirty on weekends. I left the ceiling fan running in the bedroom because I thought Gary might get overheated. He likes sleeping all bundled under the covers. I wonder if he noticed that I got a new comforter? I'd better get the coffee started. Maybe I'll cook some bacon. Weekends we like to have a big breakfast. Gary likes the smell of coffee and bacon. In this condo, you cook in the kitchen you can smell it all over the apartment. It makes you think twice about what you cook if anybody is coming over. I've been having these night sweats.

I saw Dr. Hobart last week. She said, "It will pass." She also said it sometimes hangs on longer with some women than with others. I hope I'm a short-termer. It's not like it's a constant. The flashes come and go. Gary hasn't said anything, but I'm sure he knows what's going on. I'm fifty-two. Not a bad looking fifty-two (if I say so myself). A little grey sneaking in along the hairline, but I'm so blond it doesn't stand out. I don't know what Gary thinks. I suppose he thinks I'm holding together okay. He still reaches across to my side of the bed for the occasional roll in the hay, though not lately (thank God). Can't imagine the heat of the moment mixing well with the heat of "the change." Gary turned sixty last month; he could be having problems of his own – that prostate thing. I worry about him. He could stand to lose a few pounds. I watch what he eats at home but I know he's woofing down burgers and fries when he's at the office. Now that his little princess – our daughter, Trish – has her MBA from Wharton maybe he'll ease up on work a bit and we can take up a few activities that will provide him with a little more exercise. Maybe I'll suggest it – over bacon and coffee.

He

I smell bacon. Kate probably has bacon and eggs and home fries ready. She used to make scrambled eggs or omelets, but now she poaches the eggs. I guess that makes them better for me and for this little paunch I've developed. Well, it's not so little, so maybe the poaching is a good thing. Of course, I still wolf down plenty of bacon and home fries, so measuring the benefits of poached eggs is difficult. I suppose I could eat less, but Kate goes through so much trouble with these Saturday breakfasts. I wouldn't want her to think I don't appreciate it. Then, maybe she does it because she thinks I expect it. I should just ask her. She'd probably appreciate my losing a few pounds. She looks so good. She could easily be mistaken for Trish's older sister whereas I would never be mistaken for anyone other than her father. I'm fine with that. I don't want to look younger – just better. I have this blue blazer that Kate bought for me about ten years ago. I love that blazer. It's hanging in the closet waiting for the day that I can wear it without hunching my shoulders forward and forcing the button into it's hole. Okay, starting today it's easy on the home fries and bacon (and the brioche). That blazer is going to see active duty. Every time I wore that blazer it was like having Kate's arms wrapped around my body. I don't think I ever told her that. Maybe I'll tell her when she asks me why I'm not eating more. She will ask.

She

Two pieces of bacon? No butter on the brioche? What is he not telling me? He had his yearly physical last month. He said everything was fine. But would he tell me if it weren't? Sometimes Gary's misplaced machismo can be a little irritating. He doesn't want you to think there is anything he can't handle. If he were diagnosed with cancer he would most likely keep it to himself until I caught him throwing up from the chemo. I went back to teaching elementary school when Trish was in seventh grade. She didn't need me around anymore and I needed to get back to being something other than Trish's mother. The hardest part of going back to teaching? Convincing Gary that I was doing it because I wanted to, not because I thought we needed the money – though the extra money did come in handy when Trish went to college. Can I tell you how much it costs to go to Wharton these days? I love teaching. I'm good at it. I don't know how many teenage minds I could inspire but my second graders love me. Gary is trying to make it look as though he's eating more than he actually is. I'm being hyper. He's probably just decided to take off a few pounds. I hope that means he's eased up on the burgers and fries. What am I saying? Look at what I'm feeding him. Brioche? Home fries? You're not thinking, Kate. Didn't you – just last week – ask him why he didn't wear that blue blazer anymore? He doesn't wear it because you're stuffing him with home fries and brioche. The damn jacket probably doesn't fit.

He

Want to catch a movie tonight?

She

Sounds good. Maybe we should catch a late afternoon showing then go out to dinner.

He

Sounds good. You wont have to cook.

She

I don't mind cooking.

He

Why bother? We can try that new Italian place.

She

What new Italian place?

He

That place Trish mentioned…on Ninth Street…near the Italian market. You feel like pasta?

47

She

I could do Italian. Then again, it's Saturday. Saturday night is probably not the best time to try a hot new restaurant.

He

I don't think it's that. Trish described the food as good, filling and inexpensive.

She

Still, it's Saturday. The market will be crowded, so the restaurants will be busy.

He

It's Saturday all over. Any restaurant in Center City will be busy – any restaurant that's any good.

She

That take out place is just two blocks from the theater. We can pick up a rotisserie chicken and eat here.

He

So, we're going to the movie theater across the street? Something there you want to see?

She

You mentioned that you wanted to see that new Julianne Moore film. What's it called? Alice something...or something Alice? It's playing across the street. I could do that.

He

You could or you want to?

She

So, we'll do chicken and salad?

He

I knew she'd ask. 'Two slices of bacon?' Just as well. Now she knows I'm trying to be good about the calories. Next weekend she wont feel the need to go thru so much trouble. We can do granola and yogurt for breakfast. Saturday mornings should be sleep-ins for her too. Dealing with those second graders is no piece of cake, though I think Kate really likes teaching. Personally, I could stand to work a little less. Kate has the summers free. We could do some traveling. Bum around Europe for a month, no set schedule, no deadlines. But that might not appeal to Kate. Kate's a planner. (Did I mention that before?) I wouldn't be surprised if all teachers were planners (the good ones, anyway). I should have suggested another movie. I think this one is about early onset Alzheimer's. Kate probably isn't interested in seeing Julianne Moore slip into dementia. I think they may be about the same age. Something more upbeat might be more appropriate Saturday night entertainment. I hope she wasn't ruling out that Italian restaurant because of the pasta. No way I'm giving up pasta. Not even for the comfort of my blue blazer.

She

The rotisserie chicken will be so much easier than dealing with a restaurant after the movie. Going out to eat on a Saturday night has become such a production. Everybody and their brothers pile into the center city restaurants. If you don't have a reservation, forget it. (That's if the restaurant even takes reservations.) "There's about a forty-minute wait, but you can hang out at the bar and we'll call you." Screw that. (I know. That's no way for a second grade teacher to talk. Well, screw that, too.) If we're not going to eat out I could just make lasagna and we could heat it up after the movie. Gary loves pasta. We should visit Italy. We've never been. We've talked about going. We've talked about going lots of places. Maybe we'll travel a bit now. People think teachers spend their summers seeing the world. Not if you've got a family. Our summer vacations were always ten days in a rented cottage in Cape May. Every August the three of us would pack up and head for the Jersey shore. It was nice. Trish loved it, even when she was a teenager. The summer after Trish finished her sophomore year of college was the last August we rented the cottage. We haven't really taken a vacation since. A weekend here and there, but that's it. That will change now. No more college bills. I know Gary would like to travel.

He

Kate, remember that cottage we used to rent in Cape May?

She

Of course, I remember.

He

I always liked that cottage. Not fancy, but comfortable. And Cape May was nice.

She

Really nice. Cape May, I mean. The cottage was nice too.

He

We should go down for a week this summer; see what the place is like now.

She

We could do that. We don't need to go back to the cottage. Without Trish I can't imagine needing the extra space. We could do a B and B or that old Victorian hotel.

He

Yeah. That would be good. With the cottage, you would want to cook. Wouldn't be much of a vacation.

She

I never minded cooking. We ate out a lot when we were there.

He

I know. I know. Having the kitchen was a real convenience when Trish was little. Hey, maybe you want to go someplace completely different.

She

Like…?

He

I don't know. We could go on a cruise.

She

A cruise? You want to go on a cruise?

He

I don't know. What about you? Cruising sound appealing?

She

A cruise to where?

He

I don't know. Where would you like to go?

She

It was your idea. You must have some destination in mind.

He

Not really. Isn't that the thing about a cruise? It's not so much the destination as the experience of getting there?

She

I thought you wanted to go to Italy?

He

I do. We can't cruise to Italy, at least, not from Philadelphia.

She

Gary on a cruise ship? He gets nausea on a Ferris wheel. Why would he even suggest it? You think you know someone and then they zonk you with something like that. I have no interest in twenty-four-hour dining and pseudo Broadway entertainment. Although, I might find a week on the Queen Mary relaxing: dress- ing for dinner, dancing after dinner, tea and cucumber sandwiches while sitting in a deck chair, my legs covered with a soft coverlet. Is there such a thing as a coverlet? Are transatlantic crossings even like that anymore? For all I know, Cunard could be like Carnival.

He

What am I saying? Why would I even say the words 'cruise ship?' I would hate it. To keep from throwing up, I'd probably be so medicated that I'd sleep through most of the trip. We should do Italy. Fly business class. Kate would like that. It'll eat into the savings, but what the hell. What are we saving it for? Don't need to worry about Trish. With that MBA she'll make more money than I ever did. I'm glad Kate didn't hop on to that cruise ship idea. Don't know how I would have gotten out of that.

She

If we went to Italy, where in Italy would you like to go?

He

I don't know. Maybe Tuscany. It always looks scenic in the movies.

She

Which movies?

He

I don't remember which movies. But I'm sure I remember seeing movies that took place in Tuscany and it always looked scenic.

She

Scenic?

He

Yes. Scenic.

She

Cape May is scenic.

He

Not in the same way.

She

Well, I would like to go to Florence.

He

There you go. Tuscany. What could be more scenic than Florence? Cher!

She

What?

He

Cher was in the movie.

She

Cher was in a movie about Tuscany?

He

It wasn't about Tuscany. It was about something else.

What's-his-name directed it.

She

Oh, that helps.

He

You know the one I mean. Think Italian.

She

Fellini?

He

No. It's not an 'ini.' It's an 'elli.' Zeffirelli. That's it. Zeffirelli. That older actress from Downton Abbey was in it too. Of course, she wasn't so old then.

He

Maggie Smith?

He

Yeah. Maggie Smith. And Cher.

He

Oh, you mean 'Tea With Mussolini.'

He

That's it. Tuscany. Right?

She

I wonder how many times we'll have this conversation before we actually decide to book a trip? I don't know why I called Cape May scenic. I mean, it is scenic, but I don't want Gary to think I have this burning desire to return to our old habits. Not that I'm complaining about our life. It's been good – these years with Gary; and we've got a lot of years to go. It's not a crime to want them to be…different. That's why we left Jenkintown. We wanted a change. I wanted a change. Did Gary? Yes, of course he did. He wanted a change from Jenkintown and Cape May and…whatever. Going to the Jersey shore for a few days doesn't mean we're moving backwards. The sunsets were nice at the shore. I remember the time we saw a double rainbow. It was morning. Gary and I were going to the store to pick up croissants for breakfast. I saw them first – the rainbows. (Didn't want you to think I meant the croissants.) I pointed to the sky and we stood looking at these two glorious arcs, their colors slightly fuzzy as though we might be seeing them through a slight fog. Gary ran back to the house to get Trish and then the three of us just stood there…looking out to the sea and up at the sky. Trish must have been six or maybe seven years old. I remember thinking, – 'cherish this moment' – and I did. I still do. There are certain moments you can have only when your child is young. That was one of them.

He

I wonder how many times we'll have this conversation before we actually decide to book a trip? I wish Kate would just tell me where she'd like to go. I could do Italy but I'm thinking Kate is pushing it because she thinks I want to go. Her sister went to Turkey last year. She and her husband wanted us to go with them. The timing wasn't good for Kate – thank God. Her sister is called Merry. I use her full name – Meredith, because 'Merry' is such a *misnomer. If there were a name that means chronic complainer, it would be so much more suitable. Eight days touring Turkey with Meredith would surely have tried my patience. She's not a bad person, but somewhere along the line someone should have told her – if you can't say something nice…etc., etc. I've never told Kate that I can only take Meredith in small doses, but I think she knows. Her husband, Brett is okay though I do wish he'd stop trying to interest me in learning to golf. I have no interest. I grew up thinking of golf as something that old guys in lime green pants did to while away their retirement years in Florida. I've got to admit the image for the sport certainly has changed over the years. My interest hasn't. Brett taught Meredith to play. Another reason to avoid the links.*

She

Is Trish stopping by this afternoon?

He

I don't know. Wouldn't she mention it to you if she were?

She

She doesn't always tell me everything.

He

Meaning…?

She

Meaning nothing. It's just that sometimes she mentions things to you expecting you to pass them along to me.

He

Well, since I didn't pass it along you can assume she didn't mention anything to me.

She

You sometimes forget.

He

I didn't forget.

She

Just saying. Sometimes…you….

He

She might come over. What? What is that look you're giving me?

She

I'm not giving you a look.

He

You think she said something to me and I forgot to tell you. She didn't. I'm just thinking she needs to get the rest of her stuff. She's been in her new place for three months now. There must be stuff in those boxes she left in the hall closet that she needs.

She

I doubt it. We're just a convenient storage place until she decides she can toss it all. You should tell her that we'd be happy to get rid of it for her.

He

I should tell her?

She

I'm glad I went back to teaching. I'm much better dealing with twenty-two second graders than I ever was dealing with one daughter. I wouldn't call Trish a mistake, but she wasn't planned. I should have gone back to work sooner, but Gary was so happy being a daddy and a husband and a provider. Trish moving into her own place was a big deal for him. For me – not so big. Don't get me wrong. I love my daughter, but Gary and I need to be just 'us' for a while. I need to stop thinking that if we were in a burning building Gary would save Trish and yell to me – "Come on."

He

I don't know why Kate thinks Trish tells me things she doesn't tell her. Oh, there was a time when I thought my little princess would always be daddy's little girl but I'm noticing a closeness to her mother as Trish gets older that makes me think I'll one day be on the outside looking in, unable to be a part of whatever the two women share. Kate didn't want to be a stay at home Mom, but she did it. I don't think I've ever thanked her for that, and I should, because I'm pretty sure she did it for me.

She

Let's go for a drive. It's a nice day. Let's go up to New Hope.

He

What about the movie?

She

If we get back in time, we'll go. If not….

He

We'll just play it by ear.

She

Yeah. That's it. No plans. Sometimes unplanned things can bring you the most joy.

He

Yeah?

She

Yeah.

I Just Always Thought There Would Be More

I know this was my choice and it's only been two weeks, but it seems so unfinished – my life. Things that I could have done… should have done. I'd include 'would have done,' but that implies I had a reason for not doing. I always said I wouldn't be a burden to anyone. Made it clear that if I couldn't take care of myself then I just wanted to be put someplace where people were paid to take care of me. The kids, the grandkids – they need to be able to get on with their lives, now that mine is nearly over. I suppose it's nearly over. I guess you can hang on for quite awhile in these places. I mean it's not like I'm feeble. I'm mobile. Hell, if Jess were still alive I'd still be at home, sleeping in my own bed. Dumb luck – her getting that crazy cancer.   I was supposed to be the first to go. We agreed on that. And it should have worked out that way considering that she gave up smoking ten years ago while I still sneak puffs on those killer sticks every chance I get. Forty- three years of marriage and then I'm figuring out how to go it on my own. Made it through eight years then I just started to go downhill. But maybe I've been going downhill for a long time. Jess and I – we always used to talk about what we were gonna do. Plans. Dreams. 'Not now. We've got time.' Turns out we didn't. Sure, life was good. Really, life was okay, but you always thought there would be – you know – more.

Now there's not much 'more' left. If there were choices before, there sure aren't many now. "The inescapable cold of the grave or the heat of the crematorium." (Can't remember who said that, but it stuck with me.) I don't suppose the funeral parlors have a brochure that lists the most popular option – everlasting life. Unlike some of the residents here who talk about being 'ready,' I would check the everlasting life box, though I would like Jess to be here to share it. Hell, I don't mind being old; I just don't want to be dead.

Sandra – she's our oldest – Sandra helped me move into this place. Wilson – her younger brother – he came to visit that first weekend. No visitors since then. But that's the point, right? If they have to keep running here to check on me I might as well be at home. Sunny View is home now. Why the hell they call it Sunny View is beyond me. I guess it gets its fair share of sun but the view from my side of the building is mostly New Jersey highway. I can see one of those traffic circles about a quarter mile up the highway. Who in blazes thought those up? You miss your cut-off and you have to drive all the way around the damn circle to get back to where you want to go. The alternative? I don't know. I just know that I'm one of the damn fools that end up going around the circle more than once.

Jess would hate this place. One day of eating what's on the dining room menu – or more likely, not eating – and she would be out of here. Been here over two weeks and I haven't had a vegetable that hasn't been cooked longer than Joan of Arc. If you asked Jess how she likes her broccoli she'd say 'green.' That's because her mother used to cook it until it turned gray. The cooks here at Sunny View are of the same culinary school as Jess's mother. Broccoli, green beans, carrots - all have the life cooked right out of them. Kind of like some of the residents. The life is cooked right out of them. I've got to avoid that.

Sandra and Wilson will probably drop in next weekend. Grandkids might even come with them. I've got two. Tarabithia – yeah, you read right – 'Tarabithia' – is Sandra's eighteen-year-old. She's in her first year at Rutgers. Smart girl. Calls herself "Tara." (Told you she was smart.) Wilson's boy, Robert wanted to take a few years to find himself after graduating from high school. It's been three years and he's still searching. Has no idea what he wants to do with himself.

If Sandra comes I hope she doesn't bring Oscar. My daughter's husband is a very nice man, but a little hard to take sometimes. He's a very 'take charge' kind of guy. The last thing I need in this place is someone pissing off the attendants and nurses telling them how to do their job. Visitors get to go home. Residents have to stay and suffer the attitude of the pissed off staff. Wilson can bring his wife Ada. The most Ada will do is mention that my pajama bottoms don't match the tops. Ada gets along really well with her son Robert.

The thing about my kids visiting, I know it's because they want to. (Well, there is that 'guilt' thing, but I think I've done a pretty good job of easing them out of that.) There's no expectation that the old guy is leaving big bucks behind because Sunny View will be eating away at my savings much like caterpillars eat away at a garden – voraciously. When I learned what this place was gonna cost me I clutched at my chest and gasped. Sandra thought I was having a heart attack. If I had, she and Wilson would have gotten my savings. Instead, Sunny View will be enjoying the fruits of my labors. I should have been smart enough to transfer some of my assets, so I could have gotten a little more help from my medical insurance, but – you know – I thought there was more time.

Jess and I used to talk about spending an entire summer bumming around Europe. Jess taught third grade at Sara Roosevelt Elementary School, so she had the summers off. When you're an accountant – me – taking the entire summer off is not so easy. But then we both retired. Did we summer in Europe? You can have three guesses. (First two don't count.) We had vacations, plenty of them, but no European summer. We could have explored our artistic sides. I've got one, you know. Jess did too. You're probably thinking, 'it's not too late. Explore your artsy interests at Sunny View.' You don't want to hear my answer to that.

The thing is – after only two weeks I feel like I've exhausted all my options here at Sunny View. From here on out every day will pretty much be the same. Again, I'm here by choice. I read the brochures. I knew what to expect. But when you're making the choice you're concerned with who's pushing the pills, the physical therapy, the mattress on the bed. You don't ask if the weekly movie is more likely to feature Doris and Rock rather than Angelina and Brad. What if you don't play bridge? What if…?

What if I should have stayed at home? What if I made the wrong choice? So, I left the oven on and went to bed. A twenty-year-old could have done that. My grandson Robert could have. Yeah, I missed those last two steps and broke my left ankle. It wasn't a big deal. Well, it hurt like hell, but it was an accident. Everybody has accidents. And there is the heart thing and missing my meds, but I could have dealt. I just needed to get off my high horse and ask for a little help. But you don't want to be a burden. (Back to that. When I can't take care of myself….)

I shave every day. I dress like I've got somewhere to go. When I retired Jess took me shopping and we bought some Levis, not the baggy old guy kind, body- hugging jeans. I can still wear them.

And we got a Tommy Hilfiger blazer. I look kind of 'preppy,' but darn if those clothes don't make me feel good. If I ever want to expand my wardrobe, I'm sure Ada would be more than happy to help.

Sky diving. Walking the red carpet. Living la vie bohéme in Europe. Not gonna happen – right? But I thought they would. I still think they might (as long as I don't forget to take my meds). Can I change my mind? Do I get a 'do over?' Can I just tell Sandra and Wilson 'Hey, it was all a mistake? I'm fine. I'm going home now.' If so, I'd better do it soon or there won't be a home to go home to. Maybe I just want to be in control. I felt so helpless against Jess' cancer. Then I lost her. I lost Jess. Maybe I need to be in control, so I don't lose myself. Sandra would probably just pack up my stuff and prepare to take me home. "Whatever you want, Pops." She wasn't all that keen on my coming here, anyway. Oscar – her 'take charge' hubby – would suggest leaving at the end of the month because 'it's unlikely you'll get a refund.' Wilson might suggest a psychiatric consult. Wilson might be right.

I should give it a few more weeks. There's a trip to Atlantic City planned for the day after tomorrow. Sunny View has a recreation director who makes these things happen. I signed up. I expect most of the Sunny View travelers will spend a good deal of their time at the slots. Gambling is not one of my vices. I'm hoping for good weather, so I can kick up some sand on the beach. We'll get to have lunch at the shore. That could mean a day without mushy veggies (if we stay away from those all-you-can-eat buffets). I'll keep my fingers crossed. Good weather, good food, ocean breezes – could be a good day. But you know, I just thought there would be – more.

Being Special

Arnie Wilson was special. He had always been special. Everyone knew he was special. There was no reason to believe he wouldn't always be special. When – at the age of three – he began to speak in fully formed sentences, it was speculated that Arnie's specialness was God-given.

Selena Wilson knew Arnie was special. She knew it the first time she felt him moving in her round, taut belly. She certainly knew it when Arnie burst upon the scene a full two weeks before he was expected. Selena was sure it was Arnie's way of showing how anxious he was to be born. Dr. Peterson thought it was the lesser of several unexpecteds that could have happened, since Selena had waited till the age of thirty-eight to have her first and only child. Selena's best friend, Hilda Hynes called Arnie a special delivery. "Arnie wasn't just born. He was a special delivery." Hilda never tired of the line. Selena tired of it quickly.

Actually, the phrase was not original with Hilda. It started down at the main branch of the Allentown post office where Arnold Wilson, Sr. was a supervisor in the city mail-sorting unit. "What are you, Arnold? Forty-four? And this is your first? This kid must be a special delivery." They laughed at that one a lot in the mail-sorting room. "You hear that, Bosco? Special delivery.

That's good, huh?" Mickey Bosco, a father of four, wasn't laughing as much as everyone else.

Growing up, Arnie managed to escape most of the usual childhood diseases. It was as though he was protected by some kind of antiseptic bubble – a special immunity. Scrapes and bruises never marred his skin. He was just not prone to injury. He was a well-behaved, careful child. But there was a close call – once, when he was five years old. Arnie was riding his tricycle down the sidewalk, heading towards the wilted petunias that lined the edge of Mrs. Hynes' front yard. Just as Arnie reached the yard a small truck rounding the corner had a blowout and swerved towards the red tricycle and its innocent young navigator. Arnie should have been a goner. Hilda Hynes who was standing at the side of her house untangling a garden hose thought Arnie was a goner, for sure. Instead, only the petunias went down (and they were almost down, anyway). When Hilda ran to the edge of the yard she saw Arnie at the end of the block looking over his shoulder to see what had caused the commotion. (Sometimes, special people are oblivious to what goes on around them.) The driver of the truck was much relieved to find that petunias were the only things crushed beneath the wheels of his truck. Hilda ignored the driver's apologies, rushed down the block and wrapped her arms around Arnie.

"Arnie, you are so lucky. No, it's more than luck. You're special."

Arnie had heard his name linked to that word before. Although he wasn't completely sure of its implications, he believed Mrs. Hynes. He thought she was right. He was special. He also thought Mrs. Hynes wore too much perfume and wished she would stop pressing his face into her armpit.

People didn't notice him. Ben's mother, Beatrice Tolliver couldn't remember anyone ever bothering to peek under the hood of the navy-blue carriage she and her husband, Will, had purchased at that overpriced store over at the Whitehall Mall. She couldn't remember anyone reaching down to pinch his cheeks or scrunching up their mouth to make that kitchy-coo sound that babies are supposed to like but probably find perplexing. On those days when Beatrice found the time to sit with him in the park anyone stopping to chat seemed more interested in the origin of the carriage than in its contents. (It was an attractive carriage. The salesman at the mall had called it a 'pram' – no doubt to justify the cost – and Will and Beatrice had taken the bait.) Ben – short for 'Benton,' not 'Benjamin' – was a curious child and managed to get into…pull over…upset…and sometimes ingest many things, mainly because no one noticed him doing it.

Ben's second grade teacher – Miss Tatanacci – took her class on a field trip to Muhlenberg College to see a local theater company's production of The Wizard of Oz. Not until she was loading her charges on to the bus for the return trip to the school did she notice that Ben's handholding partner had no hand to hold. Panic stricken, Miss Tatanacci rushed back inside. There was no sign of Ben in the lobby, so she went into the auditorium. An usher was walking the aisles checking for things the children might have left behind.

"Have you seen anyone in here? I'm looking for one of my students."

"Sorry, Miss. This place is empty."

Just then the bus driver came in.

"Miss Tatanacci," he said. "I think you're looking for this one."

And there was Ben, holding the bus driver's hand. "I'm

sorry," he said. "I thought the show was boring, so I went back to the bus."

The bus driver shrugged. "I went for coffee. I never noticed him there when I came back."

Ben was an only child. Not having a brother or sister didn't bother him. He never thought about it. He liked spending time alone. He liked reading books. He particularly liked stories about people with special powers. The summer of 1974 he had his tenth birthday and Stephen King released his first book, 'Carrie.' Ben read the novel three times. He didn't have his own copy – not at first. His Mom didn't think it was appropriate reading for a ten-year-old. So, Ben went to a local bookstore where he often saw older kids hanging around and reading things without buying them and he would sit – unnoticed – on the floor between two bookshelves and read about the girl who discovered she had a very special gift. That was his first reading. When the paperback edition was released, Ben bought his own copy. (He purchased it at the same store where he had done his clandestine reading. He thought this only fair.) He kept the book in his school book bag and every night before bed he read until he had completed the novel two more times.

Arnie Wilson and Ben Tolliver were both members of the William Allen High School freshman class in the Fall of 1980. Ronald Reagan would soon be president. Pac Man would soon invade America. John Lennon would soon be killed. None of these events would greatly impact the lives of either boy. Arnie and Ben sitting side by side in Biology I lab would have an impact on many. Their being lab partners was pure coincidence since the biology teacher, Mr. Pagliacci (his real name) assigned partners alphabetically and there was no one in the class with initials between "T" (Tolliver) and "W" (Wilson). Well, actually, if Myra Sussman hadn't been out sick the day of the lab partner assignments she would probably have been Ben's partner; but since she was missing she became what Pagliacci called a 'wild card' and when she returned to class she was partnered with Charlie Zane. With Myra being absent the class was left with an uneven number of students leaving Charlie (who was a 'Z') without a partner. So, he got 'wild card' Myra. Since Myra thought Ben was a little weird but thought Charlie was William Allen High's answer to Shaun Cassidy, she thanked her lucky stars for drawing the wild card. Her little bout with the flu was quickly forgotten when she learned she would get to dissect her frog with a clone of one of the Hardy boys.

Ben and Arnie worked well as lab partners. Mr. Pagliacci often called attention to their classroom projects and complimented Arnie, telling him what a special understanding he had of the subject matter. It was left to Arnie to remind Pagliacci that he had a lab partner who contributed as much as he.

"Of course," Pagliacci always remarked. "I didn't mean to overlook Benton."

Mister Pagliacci was one of the few people that called Ben 'Benton' and Ben really wished that he didn't. Ben wanted to correct him but feared it would only call more attention to the deed.

"If I were Carrie," thought Ben, "I could just concentrate on Mister Pagliacci's lips and they would suddenly be glued together. No more calling me 'Benton.'

There was one instance when Mister Pagliacci noticed Ben – still calling him "Benton'. The class was dealing with earthworms. Ben was fascinated by the theory that earthworms could regenerate themselves. He sliced small sections off one end of his specimen until the worm was in five sections and then asked Arnie how long he thought it would take for the five sections to become five worms. Since the worms were being used in an experiment on aerating soil, Mister Pagliacci was not pleased and gave 'Benton' a lecture on the difference between curiosity and cruelty. Arnie thought Ben's experiment was kind of cool. In fact, he considered telling Mister Pagliacci that he had segmented the earthworm. Arnie felt that Pagliacci would have reacted differently had he thought Arnie did the deed. It was another perk of being special. On the other hand, Ben was surprised that Pagliacci had even noticed that he had dealt the fatal slices. Had he been working alone, the earthworm would have been segmented, observed and buried in the pile of dirt on the lab table without anyone paying any attention whatsoever to the worm or to Ben.

Over the next few months of that freshman year Arnie and Ben became confidants, though it is doubtful either thought of the other as a friend. Ben was somewhat in awe of Arnie's charmed existence and Arnie was somewhat confused by Ben's non-existence. Arnie confided how he felt that he was so lucky – special – that he often thought he could get away with doing almost anything. Ben confided that he felt the same, but only because he felt that no one would notice what he was doing. Is it any wonder they wanted to test their theories?

The newspaper coverage was not very specific. No names were mentioned. There seemed to be a lot of confusion. Nothing like this had ever happened at the Whitehall Mall. And the question on everyone's lips: "Why?" Fortunately, there were no fatalities, though one man was listed in critical condition. When interviewed by the police, Jennie Markham, a worker at one of the fast food restaurants who was just coming in for her shift said, "He just started shooting. He stood at the top of the escalator and just started shooting." Jennie gave no real description of whom she saw at the top of the escalator. No one did. The newspaper questioned: "How did the shooter go unnoticed?" That was the question. There was no answer.

Flower Children

Rose liked the idea of closed-casket funerals. A closed casket lessened the likelihood of some fool prostrating themselves over the corpse and crying – "Don't go. Don't go." – Like the body in the casket wasn't already gone. And how come so many people want to kiss a corpse? Of course, a closed casket doesn't deter the truly determined. For those who have decided their grief is uncontrollable and must be publicly proclaimed, there is no deterrent. You just have to sit there, bear it and hope the performance will be brief and not become a bid for an Academy Award.

Mabel Lewis didn't have an easy time – living or dieing. Sixty-two years old and she was gone. It was the big C that got her and it made her last days hellish. Mabel's healthy days didn't always qualify as heaven sent, what with her husband, Benny changing jobs more often than a pediatric nurse changes diapers and those two girls of theirs making them grandparents time after time without once presenting them with a son-in-law. Rose and Mabel weren't close, but she was going to the funeral because… well, because you just do. They went to the same church. They knew a lot of the same people. If Rose were being put away, Mabel would have come to her funeral.

Rose heard the side door open and close.

"Rose? Rosie? Where are you?

"Upstairs, Violet. In my bedroom."

Rose heard her sister, Violet coming up the stairs. She had just enough time to give herself a quick once-over in the mirror before Violet came into the room. She raised her hand and smoothed a few stray hairs away from her forehead and into the sleek, French twist, a style she started wearing twenty years ago and continued wearing today. A touch of color on her lips – a subtle red – was her only makeup. The simple sheath dress she wore hugged what was still a very presentable body for a sixty-year old woman. All good, though chances were Violet would have some suggested improvements.

"Rose, how many times…how many times have I told you to lock that side door?"

"Violet, don't you ever knock?"

"Don't have to if you don't lock the door. Anybody… anybody, I say could come into your house and you'd never know."

"I knew when you came in."

"That's because I made some noise to let you know I was here. A burglar or a murderer ain't gonna be that considerate."

"Well, thank you, Violet, for being so considerate."

"Don't think I'm missing your sarcasm, Miss Seditty. Just be glad I care about your well-being."

"I am, Violet. I really am."

"Why aren't you dressed yet?"

"I am dressed."

"You're wearing that purple dress?"

"It's not purple. It's more like a very dark plum."

"And plums ain't purple? Rose, I know you've got something

black you can wear to the funeral."

"Why do I have to wear black? I'm not family. I'm not even a close friend."

"You're close enough, and for a funeral, black is the most fashionable color you can wear."

"No need for me to be fashionable, just respectful. And I can be respectful in purple or blue or white or…"

"Oh m'God," Violet interrupted and sat on the edge of the bed. "Is Pansy going to show up wearing white and talking about funerals being celebrations about passing over to a better life?"

"Violet, don't start in on Pansy. She is your sister and her beliefs are not to be ridiculed."

"You know I'm not ridiculing anything. I'm as tolerant as the next person. But you know how they carry on at that church she goes to. I hope she's not planning on showing up in a white dress and carrying a tambourine…"

"Violet, stop it."

"…because she knows we don't do that kind of celebrating at our church."

"And you call me 'seditty.' Come on, Violet. Let's go downstairs. You want some coffee while we wait for Pansy and Tulip?"

Violet boosted herself off the bed and headed for the hatbox that Rose had sitting on a stool next to her closet. She set the top of the box aside and started sorting thru the hats inside. "Where's that little black pillbox hat you used to wear? It will help tone down that purple dress."

"Violet, do you or don't you want coffee?"

Violet put the top back on to the box. "I drink too much coffee." She followed Rose out of the room. "You got a pot brewin'? I don't want any of that instant stuff."

Tulip pulled up to the curb in front of Pansy's house and honked the horn of her new 1970 black Buick Riviera. She knew Pansy didn't like it when people honked their horns instead of coming up to the door and ringing the doorbell, but Tulip wanted the neighbors to see her sitting behind the wheel of her big, new Buick. Her husband wanted to get one of those small cars. He even talked about buying a Volkswagon, but Tulip had told him "Dewitt, my behind is too big to be scrunched into a Volkswagon."
Dewitt was happy to settle on the Buick when Tulip started pushing for a Cadillac. Tulip had a point. Unlike Rose and Violet who had always been on the slender side Tulip hadn't worn anything smaller than a size sixteen since she turned thirty. Both she and Pansy got the hefty genes, taking after their father who was just shy of six feet tall and weighed in at two hundred and thirty pounds. Pansy opened the door and stood with raised eyebrows looking out at Tulip. Tulip opened the car door and eased out of the driver's seat. She glanced around and caught Pansy's neighbor, Vivian Tuesdale, holding back her blue waffle-weave drapes and peeking out to see who was honking. Tulip smiled and thought, "Mission accomplished." Vivian Tuesdale would get the news out about the new Buick faster than Paul Revere spread the word about the British coming.

"You ready, Pansy darling?"

Pansy let her eyebrows slip back into place and tilted her head towards heaven. Her lips formed the words: "Help me, Jesus." She closed the door, checked to make sure it was locked and headed for the car. Without turning back she called out, " Good morning, Vivian. You going to Mabel's funeral?"

The drapes got a quick pull together and Vivian Tuesdale disappeared.

It was nearly noon and the late spring sun was riding high in the sky. Tulip got into the car. She reached into the glove compartment and pulled out a large pair of sunglasses. Putting them on she said, "Get in, Pansy. It's getting late. You like my sunglasses? Dewitt says they make me look like I'm incognito."

Pansy settled herself onto the plush leather seat. "Incognito from what?"

"You know, like I'm a celebrity or somethin'."

"Yeah, or something. Tulip, why is there so much veil on that hat? If you had any more veil you could pass for a bride."

Tulip started up the car and pulled away from the curb. "With all of this black I'm wearing nobody is hardly gonna mistake me for a bride."

"And why are you wearing pants?"

"It's a pants suit, Pansy."

"Well, a suit with a skirt might have been a better choice. We are going to church."

"We're going to a funeral. It's not the same thing."

"It's still the Lord's house."

"I thought He lived in Heaven. And as far as I can tell, the way that Reverend Stokes parades around he thinks Ebenezer Baptist belongs to him."

"Lord, have mercy."

"Don't 'have mercy' me, Miss Pansy. You know what I'm talkin' about. He is one high-minded, conceited man. That's why you and Sonny left Ebenezer and joined up over at Mount Olive. I don't know why Rose and Violet still go there."

"At least they go somewhere."

Tulip put her foot on the brake just in time to avoid going thru a red light.

The light turned green. Tulip pressed the gas pedal a little too hard and the car lurched forward pressing Pansy against the back of her seat. Pansy rarely tried to push home her religious views on others. She preferred to live by example; but Tulip was her sister and though it was true that Pansy had little respect for Stokes she thought going to Ebenezer was better than no church home at all.

Pansy and Tulip lived in West Philly where all of the sisters had grown up. Tulip drove down Chestnut Street to the 30th Street entrance to the Schuykill Expressway, which because of some badly planned entrance/exit ramps had been dubbed 'the sure-kill expressway.'

"Be careful on this road, Tulip."

"How many times have I been on this expressway, Pansy? Never had an accident, have I?"

"First time for everything."

Tulip eased into the oncoming traffic and drove the short distance to the West River Drive, cut off into the East Falls section and on into Germantown. When they arrived at Rose's house in Germantown their two sisters were sitting in the kitchen nursing cups of muddy looking coffee. Both Tulip and Pansy declined the offer to have a cup. The color of the liquid told them that Violet had a hand in the brewing and neither wanted to risk the strong dose of caffeine.

"We don't have a lot of time," Tulip prodded them. "Let's get going."

Rose took the two cups from the table and put them in the sink. "Tulip, the church is so close. We don't need to drive. We can walk."

"Don't be silly. I've got this big car. We might as well arrive in style."

"I like that suit, Tulip," said Violet. You look good in black." She cast an eye at Rose. "Your white suit is nice too, Pansy."

Rose backhanded Violet on her shoulder and spoke a little too loudly. "All right, let's get out of here. I know Violet wants to be there when the family comes in. She doesn't want to miss any of the excitement."

"Excitement?" Tulip was frowning. "Oh, Lord…"

"Don't take the Lord's name in vain."

"Sorry, Pansy." Tulip turned back to Rose. "You think there's gonna be a lot of carrying on at this funeral? I was hoping for a dignified funeral."

"There is nothing dignified about being dead, Tulip," Rose answered.

"I wouldn't be surprised at anything Mabel's girls do," said Violet. "Di Robinson told me she heard from Vivian Tuesdale that Joanie, the oldest girl asked Mister Morris at the funeral home if he would take a picture of her beside her momma in the casket."

"No." Tulip's voice registered shock, but her eyes said 'Doesn't surprise me at all.' "She wanted to crawl into the casket?"

"No," Violet went on. "She was just going to bend over the casket to get her head in close enough for the photo."

"Help me, Jesus."

Tulip turned to Pansy. "That's what Mabel's husband is going to be saying now that he has to handle those two girls on his own."

"Girls?" said Violet. "They are women."

Rose removed her sweater, a bulky, black cardigan from the back of the chair she had been sitting on. "Can we go now?"

Rose

Rose was only six months old when her parents Sephronia and Heywood Harris packed up their belongings and headed north from South Carolina to Philadelphia, Pennsylvania. The year was 1910. The Philadelphia Phillies had just won the World Series. That didn't mean much to Sephronia and Heywood. It certainly didn't mean anything to Rose. She would have no memories of that World Series. Nor would she have any memories of her few months of life in South Carolina. Had she memories, she probably would have concluded that growing up colored in Pennsylvania wasn't a lot different than growing up colored in South Carolina, at least, not while she was growing up.

Heywood had an older sister, Mavis, who had a four-room apartment on the second floor above a pharmacy. She encouraged Heywood to leave South Carolina and offered him a place to stay in Philadelphia until he could get on his feet. Mavis didn't seem to have a job, but she always had money. When Sephronia questioned Heywood about Mavis' circumstances Heywood just said 'he didn't know' and Sephronia decided it was because he didn't want to know. They stayed with Mavis for a full year. Heywood was picking up odd jobs and Sephronia was doing day's work, cleaning houses for well off white families, and they saved enough to get their own place. It was a good thing because by then Sephronia was pregnant with Pansy. Violet came along in 1915 and three years later, Tulip was born. Heywood didn't seem to mind that Sephronia kept birthing girls. He sometimes thought a boy would have been nice, but he loved his daughters and they made him happy; and all those babies probably helped keep him out of WWI. Not that Heywood would have minded being part of one of those colored fighting units, but his girls needed him more than the army did.

The place they found was a two-bedroom apartment in a four story building in Southwark. They lived there until a few months before Tulip was born and then moved to a row house with a small porch in West Philadelphia. Heywood had joined the NAACP the year before and someone he met thru a fellow member had helped him find the house, which he eventually purchased. The extra bedroom the house provided meant Rose and Pansy could have their own room and Violet would get to share with the newborn Tulip. Rose was called on to help out with household duties, but all four girls were so close in age that each shortly joined Rose, each with her own chores, though Tulip got to be the baby for a few years longer than Violet thought necessary. And, as the oldest, Rose got to be substitute mother when Sephronia had to be away from the house. It's hard to say if this duty fostered a sense of responsibility in Rose or possibly she just inherited from her father that quality that made her feel loving and protective of her family.

Rose did well in school and often helped her younger sisters with their schoolwork, especially Violet who seemed to have trouble keeping her mind on anything as mundane as addition and subtraction. Rose had thought she would like to be a teacher or a nurse, but after high school she decided she was needed at home. She took a job as a nurse's aide and lived at home until all of her sisters had graduated high school. It turned out to be a smart move. The Great Depression hit and for a while Rose became the family breadwinner. She met Willy Ford, a graduate of Tuskegee, when Tulip was a junior in high school. Willy had skin the color of burnt butterscotch and his cheeks were dotted with little brown freckles. He was tall and slender and wore wire-rimmed glasses. Rose thought he looked like a schoolteacher. She had only known him six months when he proposed. Rose held him off – in most ways – until Tulip got her diploma in June of 1936, then she and Willy were married in September. Willy had come north to practice family medicine. Unfortunately, not a lot of Negroes had money to spare for doctors. During the depression, if you had money you used it to put food on the table and hoped that would keep you healthy so you wouldn't need a doctor. So Rose and Willy wound up working side by side as nurse's aides and in his downtime Willy volunteered at a health clinic. Their son, William, Jr. was born in 1938 and their daughter, Lillian, in 1940. In the Spring of 1945, Rose and Willy found a beat up old Victorian house in the Germantown section and set about fixing it up. Willy took the first floor for his offices and except for eating – it was just too expensive to move the kitchen – they lived upstairs. It was slow going when Willy first put out his shingle, but eventually as more colored people moved into the area his practice flourished. Rose was his nurse, reception-ist and maid-of-all work. They made a good team and by the time William, Jr. was ready for college they had upgraded both the house and the offices.

Junior went off to Penn State and graduated with a degree in English Education. Lillian shared her father's interest in medicine but had no desire to spend the time necessary to become a doctor, so instead decided to become a nurse. Eighteen months into her train-ing she realized that her interest in medicine came only because her father was a doctor and she had no real interest or talent for dealing with sick people. She took a job with Bell Telephone Company as an operator, went on to become a supervisor and found she was quite happy in her new chosen field.

Once both children were out on their own, Rose and Willy settled into a comfortable routine with Willy looking out for his patients and Rose looking out for Willy. Rose remained close to her sisters. Her parents, Sephronia and Heywood moved back to South Carolina in the summer of 1954. Sephronia said she was tired of northern winters. Heywood agreed. That Thanksgiving, Rose insisted that everyone go to South Carolina. She was glad she did because less than a year later they returned to South Carolina to bury her father. Heywood – a two-packs-a-day smoker – had succumbed to emphysema. Rose tried to convince her mother to return to Philadelphia, but Sephronia resisted and only came north for graduations and special occasions. She lived to celebrate ten more Thanksgivings before a massive heart attack prevented her from getting out of bed one rainy April morning. Sephronia Harris had lived long enough to see all of her flowers blossom and grow, but it was left to Rose to weed the garden.

Pansy

Pansy loved her big sister, Rose. Though she was only two years older, Rose treated Pansy like a special doll that her parents had brought home just for her. Of course, when Violet was born, Rose had to lavish her attentions on two dolls and when Tulip joined the dollhouse, Pansy decided Rose was just not going to have enough attention to go around, so she looked elsewhere; and when she looked, she found God. Her bible-school teacher had told her that God was so great he could take care of the whole world. So Pansy surmised in her six – very nearly seven-year-old mind that God, unlike Rose, could never have his attentions stretched beyond His limits.

All of the Harris girls were sent to Sunday school and, when old enough they were required to be at the Sunday morning worship service at Ebeneezer Baptist. Pansy – at her own request

– was permitted to go to BYU, a young peoples bible study group, and up until the age of fourteen she attended summer bible school. None of her sisters chose to join her in these extra activities. As for regular school, Pansy was a good student, not exceptional, but well behaved and capable. Both teachers and students would remember her as "that girl who was always saying 'Jesus loves you.'" She sang in Ebeneezer's young people's choir. She loved the gospel songs and unlike some of the young people who made a joyful noise only because they could, Pansy truly made 'a joyful noise unto the Lord.' When she was eighteen, Pansy moved into the adult choir. Preston 'Sonny' Rawlins was also on the choir. He was six feet two, 180 pounds and resembled a young Abe Lincoln, albeit a dark chocolate Lincoln. Pansy and Sonny knew each other but they weren't really friends. Sonny was two years ahead of Pansy in school, and Sonny had an after school job so he didn't have a lot of free time. They sang together on that choir for two years, never exchanging much more than a 'good evening' or a 'how are you.' Then in 1932 a man named Thomas Dorsey wrote a song called "Precious Lord, Take My Hand." Sonny Rawlins sang solo on that song with the choir. The first time Pansy heard Sonny sing that song at choir rehearsal, she knew that if God had set aside a man for her, Sonny was that man. They were married one year later. The union produced three children: Maddie, Lucille and Walter Lee. There probably would have been more, but both Pansy and Sonny grew disinterested in using the bedroom for anything other than sleeping. Truth be told, Pansy always thought of her wifely bedroom duties as just that – a duty, much like having a hot meal ready for Sonny when he got home from the umbrella factory where he worked, first cleaning machines then as a machinist. Also, truth be told, Sonny was more interested in Pansy's pan rolls than in any roll in the hay, and after three children he felt he had been as fruitful as the Bible required.

When they married, Pansy and Sonny rented the upstairs of a row house on north Forty-ninth street. It belonged to an elderly woman who went to their church, Miss Adalyn. As far as anyone knew, Miss Adalyn had always lived alone. At eighty-two she probably decided it was a good idea to have someone else in the house. It turned out to be a lucky break for Pansy. She and Sonny had lived there only a few months when Miss Adalyn decided they should have the run of the whole house.

"I'm too old to deal with all this house," she'd said to Pansy. "I'll keep my bedroom and bath downstairs here. You and Sonny use the rest of the house as you see fit. All I ask is that you keep it clean, and keep an eye on me – make sure I'm eating and paying the bills. And, oh yes, get me to church on Sundays if I can't manage on my own."

Pansy kept the house immaculate. It took a few weeks to pull everything together. Miss Adalyn had let quite a few things go and Pansy found herself using soap and water on places and things that hadn't seen a scrub brush in some time. As for meals, Pansy cooked them all. It wasn't unusual for them to take Miss Adalyn along with them to Sunday family dinners. Indeed, they treated her like family. Even so, three years later when Miss Adalyn had a stroke and died on the way to the hospital, it came as a surprise that she had left the house and everything in it to Pansy and Sonny. Pansy went thru every envelope and box in the house trying to find a name or address of someone to contact, but in the end it was she and Sonny who sat in the front pew of the church at the funeral and mourned the loss of this lady who had adopted them as family.

The house fit the Rawlins family very well. The downstairs room that Miss Adalyn had called hers was converted back to a dining room. Maddie and Lucille had the second bedroom on the upstairs floor where Pansy and Sonny had their bedroom and young Walter Lee got the attic bedroom. Pansy and Sonny continued to be active at Ebeneezer Baptist. In 1957 the longtime minister at Ebeneezer, Reverend Wilson Davis retired and a new minister, Reverend Malcolm Stokes was brought in. Reverend Stokes and his allies on the deacon board had what Pansy thought were some pretty radical ideas about how the services should be run. He preferred what he termed a more dignified service. This made Henry Delaney the choir director smile with delight. Henry, who had a liking for snug, pin-striped suits had been trying for years to get the adult choir to sing "more high-minded music" and cut down on that "broom jumping" music. To accomplish this, he suggested having two adult choirs. The main choir would sing every Sunday and concentrate on music of his and Stokes' choosing. The second choir would only sing on special occasions and be designated the Gospel Choir. Less than a year after Stokes arrival, Pansy and Sonny decided that if they were to continue to make a joyful noise unto the Lord, they would have to do it somewhere other than at Ebeneezer Baptist, so they joined the Mount Olive Baptist congregation whose services had a much more apostolic flavor. By this time, Maddie, who had gotten pregnant and had a quickie marriage ceremony in Maryland, was living in North Philadelphia. Lucille was studying Elementary Ed at Temple University. Walter Lee was preparing to join the Air Force.

Violet

Violet liked school. She wasn't big on 'readin', writin' or 'rithmatic,' but she loved the social aspect. She would often raise her hand when teachers threw out questions to the class. She rarely knew the correct answers. She just wanted to talk. This got mixed reactions from her teachers. Some appreciated her exuberance and participation while others saw it as a bid for attention and disruptive to their teaching process. She loved performing in school pageants and plays. In elementary school she made quite an impression in a series of musical plays about healthy eating. She played Cathy Carrot, followed by Brenda Broccoli, and then – her favorite – Chiquita Banana. Chiquita was her favorite because she got to wear a yellow tutu and a big hat that looked like a bowl of fruit. The tutu was particularly important since Violet thought it was time she had not just a costume – for Cathy Carrot an orange jumpsuit and for Brenda Broccoli a green jumpsuit – but a *pretty* costume. When she reached the ninth grade she started dance classes – tap and something the teacher called 'African jazz.' Miss Penny Paton who claimed to have danced professionally in New York City had been hired by someone at the Elks Lodge – a colored fraternal organization – to teach any neighborhood child who wished to attend. Violet chose to attend and continued attending for three years. That's when Penny Paton decided she'd had her fill of Philadelphia and the Elks and whatever else she did to make ends meet and headed – presumably – back to New York City. By this time Violet had 'the bug,' and a year later when she graduated from high school (with much help from Rose) she announced that she wanted to move to New York City. Sephronia and Heywood both gave thumbs down on that idea, so Violet got a job at Miss Melba's House of Beauty. She had worked for Miss Melba on weekends all thru high school and in the summer between her junior and senior years. While working that summer Miss Melba had Violet doing more than just cleaning, organizing and putting customers under the dryer. By the time Violet started her senior year she had experience shampooing, straightening and curling hair. Miss Melba told her she had a real talent for styling and frying hair and suggested she get a license and become a beautician. When Violet asked to work in the shop after graduation, Melba thought Violet was heeding her advice, but four years later, after saving most of her wages, Violet boarded a bus to New York – destination: Harlem. At Sephronia's request, Rose and Willy were on the very next bus leaving Philadelphia for New York City. When they arrived at the Dixie Bus Terminal on Forty-second street, they found Violet sitting on a bench nursing a cup of coffee. After registering first surprise and then indignation at being pursued, Violet hugged them both and smiled for the first time since arriving at the terminal. Willy did his best to convince Violet to change her mind and come back to Philadelphia while Rose just listened. Rose knew Violet well enough to realize that the decision to return would have to come from Violet without any urging from her or Willy. So, Rose told Willy to ask a policeman for directions to Harlem; then Willy took Violet's suitcase and they headed for the subway. They got off the train at 125th Street. Without any idea where they were going, they wandered the streets of Harlem. Rose asked for directions to Abyssinian Baptist Church. She thought as long as she was in Harlem she should see the building so she could report back to Pansy. Violet wanted to see the Savoy ballroom. As it got close to sundown, Willy wanted to see some food. They asked a passerby for restaurant suggestions and were given the address of the Kingdom of Father Divine. Violet gave an emphatic thumbs-down to Father Divine and his 'angels.' She was in New York City and she wanted to have her dinner in a restaurant. They walked down Lenox Avenue until Willy saw a place that he thought looked respectable. They went in, got a table and each of them ordered the exact same meal: smothered chicken, macaroni and cheese, and green beans. Rose and Willy drank iced tea. Violet drank coffee. While they ate, they talked about what plans Violet had made about where she would live (none). What plans she had made about making a living (none). What did she plan on doing in New York? (Finally, a question she could answer.) Dance. She had saved enough money to live for at least a few months until she learned the ropes and made some connections. All during the meal Willy played devil's advocate, questioning the logic behind Violet's plans or lack thereof. Rose said little but kept her eyes on her little sister. Violet was pretty, and the emerald green in her shirtwaist dress brought out the hazel in her eyes. Her dark chocolate skin was blemish free. Her smile could light up a room. And when she talked, it was a fast, melodious sound, like listening to a jazz band singer but without the band. And she always talked that way except…except when she wasn't quite sure what was coming next, like now.   Maybe she did belong in New York City. Maybe she did belong in Harlem - or even Paris or London – but not yet.

Violet was suddenly on her feet and calling out.

"Miss Penny. Miss Penny. Over here. It's me. Violet Harris."

Rose and Willy looked towards the door of the restaurant and saw the woman Violet was hailing. She looked a little older than Rose remembered but underneath the lipstick, rouge and mascara, Rose recognized Penny Paton. She was hanging on the arm of a dark-skinned heavyset man with conked hair. He was chewing on a toothpick. At the sound of Violet's voice, he stopped chewing and started sucking on the toothpick. He turned – not just his head, but his entire body – and then his eyes traveled down the entire length of Violet's body, starting with the short bangs that lay on her forehead and continuing unchecked all the way down to her ankles.

"You remember me, Miss Penny." This came as a statement rather than a question from Violet. "I took your classes in Philadelphia. You always said that I had a lot of talent." Violet's voice had taken on that melodious sound that added to her attractiveness.

Penny Paton moved towards Violet who was still standing by Rose's chair at the table. Since she was still clinging to the arm of the heavyset man, he was forced to follow. "Wasn't your name 'Melba'?" said Penny.

"No. I worked for Melba," answered Violet. "We used to do your hair. Well, Melba used to do your hair. I helped. My name is Violet."

Penny removed her arm from the arm of her companion and without turning to him asked, "Earl, baby, be a good baby and get your Penny a Seven and ginger. Earl hesitated just long enough to remove the toothpick from his mouth and then headed for the bar. Penny noticed Rose and Willy following Earl with their eyes. "Earl is my…well I guess you could call him my manager. We girls in the business need managers."

"And what business is that, Miss Paton?" Rose asked.

Penny heard but chose to ignore Rose's question. Violet, however, volunteered: "Show business, of course."

"Yes," said Penny. "That's it, Melba."

"Not Melba," corrected Rose. "Violet."

"Of course. Violet." echoed Penny. "I know that. Don't know how I could have made that mistake. You were one of my best students." Penny turned towards the bar. "That Seven and ginger coming, Earl?"

Violet moved closer to Penny. "I'm here to pursue my career."

Penny took a quick look at Rose before she asked, "What

career is that, honey?" Rose heard just the slightest hesitation in Penny Paton's voice before she said 'honey', as though she was still making a mental choice between 'Violet' and 'Melba'. "Have you got a job in a beauty parlor here in Harlem?"

"No," said Violet. "I came to New York to be a dancer. Running into you is like fate. I could use some advice. You know, how to break into the business. Maybe I could take some more classes with you."

"Oh, I don't do any teaching, honey. Not anymore."

Earl was now beside Penny and handed her a tall glass. She took a generous swallow and said, "Tell the bartender to put in less ginger ale the next time, Earl."

"Well, maybe I don't need more classes," said Violet. "Maybe I could just start auditioning."

Penny took another swallow. "Auditioning for what, honey?"

"You know," Violet continued, "one of the chorus lines. I'll bet you know people at the clubs here in Harlem. I've never stopped practicing, so I think I'm ready."

"Yeah," said Earl. "I think you're ready."

Rose and Willy exchanged a look. Rose reached for her glass and took a sip of her iced tea. Most of the ice had melted and the outside of the glass was wet. Willy pulled a paper napkin from a dispenser on the table and gave it to Rose who wiped her fingers, then crumpled the napkin and held it in the closed fist of her right hand.

"Earl, baby, why don't you get the bartender to mix me up another Seven and ginger?" Penny raised her glass as tho she was about to propose a toast. "Remember, this time, not so much ginger."

Rose watched as Earl turned and headed back to the bar, then she opened her fist and the napkin dropped to the table.

"I'm sure I've still got the talent," said Violet. "That's not something I'd lose. Right, Miss Penny? You said I had talent."

"And you did." Penny finished her drink. "You were very good for an amateur. But as a professional…well, you may not be as ready as you think you are."

"But, Miss Penny, you said…" Violet's speech was growing hesitant, not at all melodious.

"And I meant what I said. You were the most talented girl in that class." Penny turned to Rose and Willy. "I must admit, I remember very few of the girls. The talent level wasn't very high, so Violet stood out as special." Penny turned back to Violet. "You really wouldn't make it on the line. And then there is that other problem."

"Other problem?" asked Rose.

Penny shifted her gaze back to Rose. "It's hindered my career as well, and you better believe that I can hoof it better than most of those chippies over at Small's, but unless you're high yellow, mellow yellow or cocoa tan it don't matter how high you can kick your leg."

"You're telling me my sister is too dark-skinned to be a dancer?"

"I'm telling you skin that dark would keep her out of the lines up here in Harlem even if she were the most talented dancer north of the Mason-Dixon line, which she isn't."

"No need to hurl insults, Miss, said Willy."

Violet sat down. "It's okay, Willie. It's…it's okay."

Penny swallowed the last of her drink. "I'm not insultin' anybody. I'm speakin' truth." Penny moved closer to Willy. "And if you really care about your little sister here…"

"Sister-in-law," corrected Willy.

"Whatever. If you care, you'll cart her cute little butt back to…"

"Philadelphia," Rose contributed.

"Yeah. Convince her to use the talent she's really got."

"Doing hair," whispered Violet.

"Yes, Violet. Now that I think on it, I do remember. Melba always said you had a real talent for fryin' and curlin'. Said you had 'style.' Now, way I see it, Philadelphia could probably use a girl with some style, where as Harlem is just about full up with ladies that got so much style they don't know what to do with it. Ask Earl. He'll tell you that we ladies with style are practically tripping over each other." Penny paused. She smiled at Violet. " On second thought, maybe you shouldn't ask Earl anything. Nice to see you again, honey. I need to pick up my Seven and ginger before Earl gives it away. I sure was glad to see that prohibition mess end. You all have a good trip back to Philadelphia." Penny gave a short lift of her empty glass in a half-toast to the table and made her way to the bar, to Earl and to the waiting Seven and ginger.

"I guess I don't remember much about Miss Paton," said Willy. "I only met her a couple of times. Even so, she seems changed."

"Maybe not so much," said Rose.

"I think we should go," said Violet.

"To find a hotel?" asked Willy.

"To the bus station," said Violet.

Tulip

Being the last born in a family with four girls left Tulip with plenty of hand-me downs; but by the time she was twelve years old Tulip's body had curves and a sturdiness that none of the other girls had attained at that young age so there were no appropriate hand-me-downs that would fit her. So, Tulip – the baby – often got new things. But Tulip's teenage years were the years of the great depression; so serviceable rather than fashionable was the norm. When she was younger, Tulip could count on Rose who was very handy with a needle and thread to look out for her wardrobe, but Rose's job as a nurse's aide left her with little free time for stitching outfits for the last of her dolls.

When Tulip graduated in 1936, the country was on the road to recovery but Tulip still had trouble finding a job. Pansy had married Sonny Rawlins and was living on Forty-ninth street and Rose finally tied the knot with Willy Ford after Tulip graduated, so it was just she and Violet left at the house with their parents. Violet divided her time between Melba's beauty shop and a room over at the Masonic Hall that had been used for dance classes when Violet was in high school. If the room wasn't being used, the care-taker would turn it over to Violet who would stretch and turn and jump – 'jete' she called it – keeping in shape for her planned move to New York City and a career as a chorus girl. So, it was generally just Tulip and her mother at the house when Heywood was work-ing. Rose tried to get Tulip interested in helping out at the health clinic where Willy volunteered, but after a few weeks it was clear to both Willy and Rose that Tulip needed more attention than the patients. Sephronia convinced Tulip to take a typing class and Tulip found the class to her liking. Her fingers were soon dancing around the keyboard and producing 35 words a minute, a speed she bettered by 15 words per minute with a bit more practice. In 1938 a brash, young union organizer named DeWitt Thompson was in Philadelphia working with the Brotherhood of Sleeping Car Porters. They were planning a meeting and were looking to hire a local temporary typist. Tulip heard about the job thru Violet who overheard a conversation at the beauty shop between Melba and Evelyn Waters who got the info from her husband, Moby who was a grand something-or-other at the Elks' lodge. Tulip took a bus downtown to the Brotherhood's office – a temporary rental near City Hall – and was hired on the spot. Undeniably, she was a good typist, and DeWitt's weakness for sweet-faced, full-figured ladies sealed the deal. It also sealed his fate. After four days working with and for DeWitt Thompson, Tulip decided this handsome go-getter was going to be her man. She knew there would be competition but Tulip was the youngest girl in a household with four daughters; she knew how to fight for attention. DeWitt proposed the day before Christmas Eve in 1939. They had just seen a showing of *Gone With the Wind* and had stopped off at Doc Robinson's drugstore for some ice cream. Sometime between his preaching about the racial politics of the film and his last spoonful of butter pecan he managed to slip a ring on to Tulip's finger and ask, "You do plan on marrying me, right?" They were married in the spring of 1940. Tulip didn't want just a ceremony. She wanted a wedding. Violet jumped right in as chief planner with most of her attention focused on what the bridesmaid's – the sisters – would wear. She also consulted with DeWitt about his attire and what she felt was appropriate for his best man. Tulip felt Violet spent a little more time than necessary consulting with her husband to be, but Tulip held her tongue and just observed her sister's shenanigans. Tulip did draw the line when she saw the dress that Violet wanted to wear as her maid of honor. It was red and hugged Violet's body like a mummy wrap. Tulip didn't so much object to the dress as much as she rebelled at the idea of Violet in it. Those hazel eyes, that smooth skin, those curves in that red dress…no way. This was Tulip's wedding and people were supposed to be looking at her.

Fortunately, Pansy and Rose agreed (especially Pansy). The three bridesmaids walked down the aisle in full-skirted lavender chiffon.

DeWitt's parents and his older brother Milton came down from Pittsburgh for the wedding. Mr. And Mrs. Thompson – both schoolteachers – didn't have strong feelings one way or the other about Tulip but they were glad to see their boy settle down. Although liberal in their thinking and supportive of DeWitt in his union work, they often tried to steer him in directions that would provide more financial stability. They hoped his marriage would make him see how right they were. As it turned out, DeWitt was ready to move on. The Brotherhood had secured a contract back in 1937 and DeWitt was looking for new challenges. He took a civil service exam and landed a job with the postal service in November of 1941. Three weeks later – Pearl Harbor. By February 1942 DeWitt was wearing an Army uniform and Tulip was kissing him good-bye. Through some miraculous twist of fate, DeWitt came home from the European battlegrounds with nothing more than a bum shoulder. He joined Tulip in an apartment she had rented in West Philadelphia. Tulip's typing skills had kept her working and DeWitt was able to return to the postal service. Their son, Franklin was born in 1948. Tulip was nearly thirty years old. That same year Harry Truman signed an executive order ending segregation in the military. DeWitt thought, "About time." He was probably thinking about both the executive order and the birth of his son.

Tulip never returned to the workforce after Franklin was born but DeWitt was doing well enough that he moved the family out of the apartment and into a house on Spruce Street. Tulip became the perfect homemaker, spoiling both Franklin and DeWitt and they in turn spoiled Tulip.

It was nearly five in the afternoon when the sisters returned to Rose's house.

"I can't stay long," said Tulip. "I want to be at home when DeWitt gets in."

"Tulip," said Violet, "DeWitt is perfectly capable of getting along without you hovering over him all the time."

"I don't hover, Violet. I just do what it takes to keep my man happy. I know you don't have to worry about that, but…"

"Because I've never been married?"

"I didn't say that and I didn't mean that."

"Lord knows, I've kept my share of men happy."

" Lord knows." (A quiet comment from Pansy.)

Violet headed for the coffee pot. "Well, I guess it's gonna be 'gang up on Violet' day."

"I can make a fresh pot of coffee, Violet," said Rose.

"I meant," Tulip continued, "just looking at you makes men happy."

"All of my sisters are attractive women. I come from a good-looking family."

"Rose," said Violet. "Stop acting like Mama. We're old enough to fight if we want."

"Nobody's fighting," said Pansy.

Violet turned to Pansy. "Certainly not you, Pansy. Nobody can argue with you because everything you say comes directly from on high, so arguing with you is akin to arguing with God. Right?"

Rose took a deep breath, the kind of breath that said 'How many times have I heard this before?' "Violet, sometimes your mouth takes you places your common sense should not allow you to go."

"Speaking of places people should not be allowed to go…"

Pansy interrupted. "Tulip, I know what you're going to say, and you shouldn't be critical just because the Lewis girl wanted to give her son a chance to say goodbye to his Grandmother."

"In private, thank you," Tulip answered. "That boy was much too young to be pushed up in the face of a dead person. She held that boy up to the casket and he carried on like a screaming Banshee."

"Well, Tulip," said Rose. "You can't blame the child."

"I don't. I blame the mother. And – I suspect – so did that uptight Reverend Stokes. Did you see the look on his face? The decorum" – Tulip actually said 'dee-co-rum' – "of his service was being compromised. That man wanted to boot Becca Lewis right into that casket with her mama and slam the lid."

Pansy couldn't help it. She had to laugh at Tulip's right-on-target description of Reverend Stokes.

"You ready, Pansy?" asked Tulip.

"Yes. I should go. Sonny and I have a meeting at the church tonight. We're working on a planning committee for the Spring Revival meetings."

Violet moved to Tulip. "I've got a light day at the shop tomorrow. Not many heads to do. I'll stop by before I go home if you're gonna be around."

"I'll be there, Tulip answered. "DeWitt's got a Saturday shift this week."

Violet turned to Pansy. "You know I didn't mean anything, Pansy."

Pansy smiled. "Don't lie, Violet. I don't take offense at what you said, so a lie is not necessary."

"Okay. I meant it. And you know that I was speaking the God's honest truth."

At this, all of the sisters allowed themselves to laugh. Pansy and Tulip said their goodbyes and left by the side door. Once settled in the car, Tulip said, "Vivian Tuesdale wasn't at the funeral. How many people do you think she's called about my new car?"

Rose took a package of ground beef and a package of sausage links she had picked up at the Italian market out of the refrigerator. Tonight was spaghetti night and she wanted to start the sauce. "Why don't you stay for dinner, Violet?"

Violet was still standing at the door where she had hugged Tulip when saying goodbye. Without turning to Rose, she asked, "Do you think she knows?"

"See there, Violet?" That's one of those places I was talking about. One of those places your common sense should not allow you to go."

"After all this time, I still feel…well, it was such an awful thing to do – a week before their wedding. It didn't mean anything. Not to him. Not to me."

Rose took a large pan out of the cabinet under the sink and banged it down on the stove. "Violet, stop it. If you're going to reminisce then find something worth reminiscing about. That was thirty years ago and I don't care how memorable you think you are I guarantee you that DeWitt has put it out of his mind. That man loves your sister and I doubt that he has even thought about straying since he said 'I do' in that church. So, once and for all, let it go."

Violet reached up and removed the wide-brimmed, black hat she wore and tossed it on to a chair. "Is it just you and Willy for dinner?"

"Who else?"

"Spaghetti, huh?"

"The thin kind. They call it angel hair. Willy likes to twirl it around his fork."

"Put a little sugar in the sauce like Mama used to do."

"Don't I always?"

"Too early to have a little cocktail?"

Rose pointed to the cabinet above the refrigerator. "You know where everything is."

Violet opened the cabinet and took out a bottle of Seagram's. "You got ginger ale?" She opened the refrigerator and found a large bottle of Canada Dry. She took both bottles to the table. "I wonder what ever became of Penny Payton?"

Going...Going...Gone

Picture this: tele-movie: main character returning home after being away for a long time. How long? Doesn't matter right now, but a long time. We first see this character staring out of the window of a bus. Greyhound? Maybe. Depends on the town. Thru the window we see road or scenery whizzing by. The magic of the camera makes it seem as tho the scenery (or the road) is streaming over the character's face. Then the road and the scenery become a town. The camera reads the character's thoughts "Why did I stay away so long?" Then the camera pans the main street of the town, so we can see what the character sees. Picture-book charm. And we too wonder: "Why did he stay away so long?"

Rudy walked out of the front door of the bus terminal. He saw one vacant lot, two porno shops, a party goods store, Frankie's Terminal Diner, and a pigeon in a gingko tree. If he looked up he could also see the tops of several tall office buildings, new to the city since his last visit. Picturesque in its own way, but not what Rudy came to see. He was headed for another part of town, a part of town whose urban frescos were still brightly painted on Rudy's mind. A part of town he once called 'home.'

People who grew up in cities know that time changes their old neighborhoods in ways that you don't see in the suburbs or in the country. The inner city gets discovered and abandoned and re-discovered as regularly as women's fashions. Rudy didn't expect that gentrification had advanced into his old neighborhood, but he hoped to find… well, he wasn't sure what he hoped to find. Twenty years is a long time.

His one small bag wasn't heavy, so he decided to carry it with him and check into the Holiday Inn when he came back to center city. ('Center city' was what the locals called down-town Philly.) He walked two blocks, descended the stairs to the subway and let old habits assume responsibility for getting him to the correct stop in northeast Philadelphia. A short twenty-five minutes later Rudy stood looking at streets that he had walked and crossed hundreds of times on his way to school, to play, to church. The bank diagonally across from where he stood was the bank where he had opened his first saving's account. It looked the same. Only the name had changed. The buildings around it, however, revealed no past images. Little seemed to be untouched by time. The movie theater where he had spent so many hours viewing the days and emotions of oversized celluloid figures, none of whom could ever be aware of the repetition of their lives, was now a mini-mall whose marquee flashed "Bargains Galore." Both sides of the street were dotted with generic stores just as they had been when Rudy was a child, but more…, well, 'tacky' was the word that came to mind. At least they seemed so thru his adult eyes.

Rudy walked away from the commercial strip and headed down the street towards the block where his family had lived. A woman approaching was smiling at him. Rudy searched his memory, but no name came forth to identify the smiling face.

"Rudy? I thought that was you. Why, where you been?

We don't ever see you around here anymore. But I hear about you. Hear you're doing really well. "Her cherry red lips stopped forming words and pursed for a few seconds before continuing. "I'll bet you don't even know who I am."

"Of course, I do," Rudy lied.

"Just 'cause you don't have family here anymore don't mean you can't come back to visit. Come to church some Sunday. Everybody'd be so glad to see you. 'Course, it ain't like it used to be. Not so many young people anymore. You remember my daughter, Brenda? She's working downtown. Works for the city. Good job, but she's always talkin' bout changing. I tell her to think twice. Good jobs with all those benefits don't come along too often. She just got divorced. You ought to call her. She'd be glad to hear from you. You all used to hang out together in high school."

Rudy thought, "Brenda?" I did go to high school with a 'Brenda.' What was her last name?"

"I've got to get on up to the bank before it closes," the cherry red lips continued. "You remember not to be such a stranger. You're lookin' really good, Rudy. You take care."

"Thanks," Rudy replied. "You do the same. And say hello to Brenda...Mrs. Loomis."

Rudy was thankful for the last-minute memory jog. Mrs. Loomis' face registered no surprise. She had believed he remembered her all along.

Rudy continued walking. How could such familiar streets seem so foreign? Buildings that seemed to pulse with life when he was a child now sat quiet and tired. Some were empty. Some were gone. He passed Miss Maisie's house, Miss Maisie who always gave him a dollar to carry her groceries. He would have carried them for her without the monetary incentive. He liked Miss

Maisie. She always looked nice – her clothes crisp and clean, her hair in place. And she smelled nice; like the wild roses that grew in her garden.

"Don't get stuck here, Rudy," she would say, and Rudy would wonder why she stayed if it was such a bad place to be. He wouldn't ask, but he wondered. Now he looked at the house. A child looking out from the enclosed porch held up his toy truck for Rudy to see. Rudy smiled and gave the boy a 'thumbs up.' How long since Miss Maisie died? The people living in the house now hadn't kept it up. It was badly in need of a paint job. But the wild roses were blooming. Like Miss Maisie, they refused to give in to their surroundings.

"You've got to have a little pride, Rudy." Miss Maisie's voice was clear in his thoughts. "Respect yourself or nobody else will. Don't let anybody tell you different. Set your own standards and set them high. A person needs something to reach for. Reaching high is what keeps us out of the gutter."

Rudy was close to the street where his family had lived, right around the next corner. Two teenage boys stood at the corner. A car pulled over to the curb and one of the boys walked over to talk to the driver. Rudy walked past the car and heard his name.

"Rudy? Man don't you walk past this car without speakin' to me."

Rudy moved to the car window and the boy moved away. The man inside continued talking.

"That's right. It's Benny Wilson, so don't even try to walk on by without stoppin'."

"Benny!" Rudy bent to the window. "I'll be damned. Man, how you doin'?"

"Good, bro. Real good." Benny pointed towards the boy who

had talked to him. "That's my boy, Carl. You remember, me and Connie got married." Benny leaned in towards Rudy and whispered. "Carl was the reason." No longer whispering, Benny called to his son. "Carl, this is Rudy. We grew up together. "

Rudy turned to see the boy nodding and giving some unintelligible greeting.

"He's a good-looking boy, Benny. Must take after his mother."

Benny laughed. "You around for long?" he asked. "Probably just passing thru, huh?"

"Yeah," Rudy answered. "Just passing thru."

"Well, I gotta go pick up Connie at the A&P, then I gotta get back to work. I'll see you around, man."

Benny drove off. Rudy wondered what kind of job allowed Benny time off to pick up his wife at the A&P. Carl and the other boy mumbled something and walked off. Rudy returned the mumble and walked around the corner. It occurred to him that it was Thursday. He looked at his watch – one-thirty. Shouldn't Carl be in school?

Rudy now stood on his street, his block. Herman Rosen's hardware store still stood on the corner, but the sign no longer read "Rosen's Hardware"; instead, it shouted "LAUNDROMAT." Rudy had worked for Mr. Rosen one summer. He was a nice man. He lived upstairs above the store and he had a huge garden in back of the store. His daughter, Amy, was always trying to get Mr. Rosen to give up the store and move to Florida, but Herman Rosen liked his store and his garden, and after his wife, Emma, died he rarely strayed from either. Rudy wondered if Amy finally got her wish, selling the store and sending Mr. Rosen off to sit in the sun and have early bird dinners. Perhaps Mr. Rosen prevailed, holding out until he could go to Emma instead of going to Florida. He stood for a moment staring at the Laundromat. A young woman came out pulling a two-wheeled cart. An overstuffed laundry bag sat uncomfortably in the cart. After maneuvering her way thru the door, she got behind the cart and pushed it up the sidewalk, and Rudy wondered, 'where do people go to get all those things that Mr. Rosen used to sell in his store?'

A few doors down was Jimmy Preston's house. It seemed to be the only building in the block that looked unchanged. Even the curtains in the windows – lacey and slightly off-white in color – looked like the same curtains Jimmy's mother washed and rehung every Monday. Perhaps she still performed this ritual hanging. Perhaps Jimmy still lived there. Next to the Prestons' was the Johnsons', then the Tylers' then what should have been the house where Rudy grew up, but it didn't look right. It didn't look right at all. Rudy stood at the corner looking across the street at the three-story row house. The window frames he remembered were a forest green, now they were a non-descript brownish color, and where window boxes had perched with wide mouths waiting to receive their yearly springtime feast there was nothing save a makeshift television aerial hanging precariously from a second story window. The house next door was boarded up. It all looked foreign, not at all familiar. Rudy wanted to move closer; wanted to peek into the living room, to see the cramped space his mother filled with furniture too large to sit comfortably in its surroundings; wanted to look up at the top floor window where he spent so much of his time reading, and the room beyond where he slept and dreamed.

"Rudy, what are you doing up there?"

"Nothing, Mom. I'll be down in a minute."

He wanted to move closer, but he didn't. Someone came out

of the Preston house. Was it Jimmy? Rudy was close enough to see that the face was right. It was older, of course, but it was Jimmy's face. The body was heavier now, maybe as much as forty pounds heavier. Was he visiting his mother, or did he still live there? Rudy thought it was probably the latter and the thought made him feel bad. He was relieved when Jimmy headed off in the opposite direction. They were never really friends and conversation would have been awkward.

Rudy didn't want to be here. He couldn't remember why he had felt the need to come at all. Whatever had been good for him here had faded long ago and it would take more than a Greyhound bus to bring it back into focus. He turned away and retraced his steps back to the subway. He passed Carl who was standing on another corner. Neither he nor Carl bothered to mumble a greeting. No need to check into the Holiday Inn. There should be a bus leaving soon.

creative

donkersey.com